God's
greatest
Gifts

God's greatest Gifts

10 REASONS TO REJOICE

R. DEVAN JENSEN

CFI
SPRINGVILLE, UTAH

ISBN 13: 978-1-59955-333-7

Published by CFI, an imprint of Cedar Fort, Inc., 2373 W. 700 S., Springville, UT 84663
Distributed by Cedar Fort, Inc., www.cedarfort.com

LIBRARY OF CONGRESS CATALOGING-IN-PUBLICATION DATA
Jensen, R. Devan, 1967-
  God's greatest gifts / R. Devan Jensen.
    p. cm.
  Includes bibliographical references.
  ISBN 978-1-59955-333-7
  1. Providence and government of God--Mormonism. 2. Gifts, Spiritual--Church of Jesus Christ of Latter-day Saints. I. Title.

  BT135.J46 2009
  231'.5--dc22

  2009043196

Cover design by Angela D. Olsen
Cover design © 2010 by Lyle Mortimer
Edited and typeset by Melissa J. Caldwell

Printed in the United States of America

10 9 8 7 6 5 4 3 2 1

Printed on acid-free paper

Every good gift and every perfect
gift is from above.

—JAMES 1:17

CONTENTS

Acknowledgments

First and foremost, I am grateful for God's greatest gifts, especially the gift of His Only Begotten Son. Deepest gratitude also goes to my wife and children for putting up with an absent-minded husband and father, who often wandered around the house with a vacant expression, only to exclaim, "Aha!" and revise the manuscript once again.

Thanks go to Val Hawks, Richard Neitzel Holzapfel, Stewart Hughes, Stephen Lesser, Barbara E. Morgan, Brent R. Nordgren, Joany O. Pinegar, Rosalind E. Ricks, Ted D. Stoddard, and Stanley J. Thayne for reading early versions of the manuscript. Thanks also to Melissa Caldwell for her editorial expertise, to Angela Olsen, who provided the design, and to Lyle Mortimer for the opportunity.

Finally, thanks to all my dear friends and colleagues at Brigham Young University. What a joy it is to work with people who love the Lord, who follow in His footsteps, and who care deeply about each other! It is good to be a laborer in Zion.

Introduction:
The *Greatest* Gifts

About ten years ago, I worked as a copy editor at the *Ensign* magazine. While there, I proofread talks for the conference issues of the magazine. What a joy it was to read through the words of living prophets and apostles—and to get paid to do it! I testify that their words are modern scripture, representing the will of the Lord, the mind of the Lord, the word of the Lord, the voice of the Lord, and the power of God unto salvation (see D&C 68:4).

One day while proofreading, I was surprised to note that many General Authorities had referred to several gifts of God as "the greatest." For example, Elder Alexander B. Morrison of the Seventy wrote, "At this season of gift giving and gift receiving, this season of rejoicing in the great gifts that our Heavenly Father and Jesus Christ have given us, it is most fitting to ponder their *greatest gift of all*—the gift of life."[1] Of course, I saw wisdom in that statement, because the gift of life allowed us to receive a body and the blessings of seeing, hearing, smelling, tasting, and feeling.

Then I read a statement by President Gordon B. Hinckley, who said, "On Calvary's hill [the Savior] gave His life for each of us. That is the *greatest gift* that any of us can ever receive. It is the gift of the

Resurrection and eternal life."[2] I certainly agreed with that statement as well. Christ gave His life for us so that we could be resurrected and receive eternal life, returning to the presence of the Father. What greater blessing could we receive?

Later I read the words of President Wilford Woodruff, who told Church members that though "you may have the administration of angels, you may see many miracles, . . . I claim that the gift of the Holy Ghost is the *greatest gift* that can be bestowed upon man."[3] That idea resonated with me because I have been grateful for the guiding and protecting influence of the Holy Ghost.

I decided to run a computer search and identified at least ten solid possibilities:

- *The Gift of Life*
- *The Gift of the Plan*
- *The Gift of God's Son*
- *The Gift of the Resurrection*
- *The Gift of the Holy Ghost*
- *The Gifts of the Spirit*
- *The Gift of Healing*
- *The Gift of Forgiveness*
- *The Gift of Grace*
- *The Gift of Eternal Life*

As I researched, I realized that the label of "greatest" depended on which gift was being emphasized. It finally dawned on me that all the gifts of God might collectively be called the greatest—much like a "greatest hits" album by a favorite artist. These greatest gifts surpass any of the garden-variety gifts we offer each other on birthdays or special holidays. The gifts of God are eternal in nature, reflecting the benevolence of a merciful Creator. Notwithstanding all this discussion, I believe one gift does qualify as the greatest, even the gift of eternal life (see D&C 14:7).

I invite you to join this quest to better understand God's greatest gifts. I promise that as you ponder each of His gifts, you will feel a renewed sense of gratitude for His tender mercies—I did, and you will too. I hope this book will make you laugh and cry and, above all, reflect on the goodness of God. Finally, I pray that the Lord's Spirit will fill you with hope and courage—not only to survive the challenges of mortality but also to thrive in those conditions.

NOTES

1. Alexander B. Morrison, "Life—the Gift Each Is Given," *Ensign*, Dec. 1998, 15; emphasis added.

2. Gordon B. Hinckley, "Inspirational Thoughts," *Ensign*, Feb. 2007, 6; emphasis added.

3. *Teachings of Presidents of the Church: Wilford Woodruff* (Salt Lake City: The Church of Jesus Christ of Latter-day Saints, 2004), 48; emphasis added.

1. The Gift of *Life*

"What doth it profit a man if a gift is bestowed upon him, and he receiveth not the gift? Behold he rejoices not in that which is given unto him, neither rejoices in him who is the giver of the gift."
—DOCTRINE AND COVENANTS 88:33

Once there was a grumpy man. On the outside, he appeared happy enough. He tried to be patient. He served faithfully in the Church. He was pleasant most of the time, and he even whistled while he worked. But inside he was sometimes miserable because he was such a perfectionist.

You know the type. When a perfectionist teaches Relief Society, she color coordinates the tablecloth with the handouts. When she visit teaches, she loses sleep if she falls short of 100 percent.

Well, this man fretted and stewed because he wanted his life and his family to be extraordinary. He wanted his wife to be model-perfect and the children to be perfect little angels, who earned straight A's in school, never quarrelled, never shouted, did their chores without complaining, and went to bed right on schedule every night. He wanted his home to be neat and tidy and orderly, with everything in its proper place.

Now, as everybody knows, the real world is a messy place where cars break down and homes need repairing. Scientists call this "entropy," the tendency for things to move toward a state of disorder. If you have children at home, you understand this concept. Sometimes the gap between the ideal and the real can be frustrating. It was for this man. Sometimes he got upset when the home was messy. Sometimes he felt disappointed when the children complained about doing chores or doing homework or going to bed before midnight on a school night. Sometimes he felt frustrated when things did not go well at work.

Whenever life fell short of his expectations, he kept disappointment bottled up like an overheated radiator—after all, he was supposed to be a Saint. But he felt unhappy. He fretted about his imperfect home, his imperfect family, and his imperfect life.

One day a wise friend shared a bit of counsel. He talked about how each night before he went to bed, he would take a few moments from the rush of everyday life to ponder the question, "Have I seen the hand of God reaching out to touch us or our children or our family today?"[1] This friend would search his memory for evidence of God's blessings in his life, taking time to record those blessings in his journal. And as he did so, small miracles that had been overlooked in the rush of the day would become obvious to him. Like a detective, he found clues that the Lord was with him, giving him reason to believe the Lord intimately understood his circumstances and continued to guide him quietly through his challenges. As he recorded these small and simple blessings, the Holy Ghost whispered peace to his soul.

The simple advice to acknowledge the hand of the Lord changed the life of the miserable man, inspiring him to find evidence of God's hand in his life and to find greater joy in the journey. He learned to accept imperfection as part of mortality. He learned to be grateful for the gifts of God, both big and small. As he noticed the gifts of God showered on him every day, the little flaws in his home or family life no longer seemed so important. He learned to accept and love his family members, flaws and all. And they, in turn, seemed more ready to accept his many flaws! He felt a renewed sense of confidence in God's ability to work things out in the long run.

In case you missed it, the grumpy man was me. Well, confession is good for the soul! The fact is, we all are flawed disciples and need to show patience toward one another, but I believe this story of grumpiness is all too common—in many settings and many languages. As mortals, we have a natural tendency to want more than we have. Unfortunately, sometimes we get stuck in the same old rut of covetousness, and we say, "Poor Me" (with a capital M), and our hearts shrink like the Grinch's, becoming two sizes too small.

Stuck in Our Own Story

A friend of mine wrestles with anxiety and depression. Though his affliction has a biological component, he filters everything through a negative lens. Blessed with a loving, patient wife and adorable children, he nevertheless spends countless hours losing himself in a virtual world of online games and chat rooms. Blessed with the knowledge of the restored gospel, he digs into the latest conspiracy theory with relish, enjoying a life of doubt rather than faith. Some months ago, he bore testimony of the restored gospel in sacrament meeting and then, in the foyer immediately afterward, voiced serious doubts about the honesty of Joseph Smith. He did not seem to realize the fundamental disconnect between testifying of the Prophet and then tearing him down a few moments later. My friend complained about being fired because his employer "could not handle the truth." I felt frustrated with this statement because I knew the greater problem was his negative outlook on life and on others around him. It was as if he was tired of not living up to his own standards, and he wanted to take others down with him.

Amanda Dickson, cohost of the morning news radio show on KSL, described a friend who complained constantly. With slumped shoulders and a downward gaze, he complained about his current assignment. When he was promoted, he griped about his new expanded duties. He kept complaining until the day they fired him. When he asked his supervisor why he was being let go, the supervisor said it was largely due to his negative attitude. He didn't listen. When he talked to the general manager, the manager deferred to personnel. When he finally asked Amanda why he was being let go, she almost told him, "It's because of you. You got fired because you drained the energy and passion from everyone you encountered, and no business can afford that kind of loss of resources." Instead, the best answer she could muster was, "It may not have been fair, but if you really want to know the answer—you've got to look inside." Watching his reaction, she commented, "I don't think he heard me."[2]

Like Amanda, I have seen many, especially those who consider themselves victims of tragedy—either real or imagined—get stuck in their own story. They tell the juicy details to any who will commiserate. Misery truly loves company.

Why do we stay stuck in our own story? I believe it's because it's easier to put the blame on others than to take personal responsibility for our own happiness.

But it's a gloomy half-life to live in misery while blaming others for our unhappiness. To all those in this situation, I share these seven words: "When—the—horse—is—dead, GET—OFF!"[3] Sometimes we ride that dead horse until it starts to stink. It doesn't matter whether it is a failed relationship, the loss of a loved one, or a frustrating job. Whatever it is, get off and get moving!

The very heart of the gospel is the infinite Atonement of Jesus Christ, which offers us power to break from our cocoon of misery and transform us into new creatures. Indeed, the word *repentance* means "a change of mind" and "a fresh view about God, about oneself, and about the world." In other words, the transforming power of the Atonement helps us see with new eyes the tender mercies of the Lord in our lives and take hold of hope to get out of bed each morning. In the face of real challenges, the Atonement offers us real hope, real peace, and even good cheer. This power is available to us not only in the good times but also, and especially, in the bad times.

Be of Good Cheer

The Lord repeatedly counseled his disciples to "be of good cheer" and "be not afraid" (Matthew 14:27). Based on recent teachings of our living prophets, seers, and revelators, the words "be of good cheer" appear to be as much a commandment as an invitation. When we are tempted to gripe about our lots in life, Elder Jeffrey R. Holland reminds us to "speak hopefully" and "speak encouragingly, including about yourself." In other words, let's look for the positive in each situation. Then he adds this sage advice: "No misfortune is so bad that whining about it won't make it worse."[4]

Life is a struggle—it was meant to be so. But we were meant to find joy along the way—joy in the journey. We are invited to press forward with "steadfastness in Christ" and "a perfect brightness of hope" (2 Nephi 31:20). That does not mean we gloss over the trials of life. Exercising hope in Christ does not mean we cannot handle the truth or that we have a Pollyanna attitude, thinking this is the best of all possible worlds. But it does mean that we exercise faith that if we do our part, Christ will be at our right hand and our left and will send His angels to bear us up (see D&C 84:88). Faith means that we put our trust in God that He will right all wrongs, even when some wrongs will not be righted until Judgment Day.

Sometimes life knocks you down, and then, as you are standing up, it knocks you down again. I am not suggesting that you overlook life's unpleasant aspects; instead, face them with courage and a healthy sense of optimism—a pervasive sense that things will work out in the long run.

I love this quote from Elder Orson F. Whitney: "The spirit of the gospel is optimistic; it trusts in God and looks on the bright side of things. The opposite or pessimistic spirit drags men down and away from God, looks on the dark side, murmurs, complains, and is slow to yield obedience."[5]

Certainly we saw that sense of optimism in President Gordon B. Hinckley, who believed in the motto "Things will work out." He liked to say, "If you keep trying and praying and working, things will work out. They always do. If you want to die at an early age, dwell on the negative. Accentuate the positive, and you'll be around for a while."[6] He certainly seemed to take his own advice.

Regarding the need for courage to face the challenges of life, one poet wrote,

> It is easy enough to be pleasant
> When life flows by like a song,
> But the man worth while is one who will smile

6

When everything goes dead wrong.
For the test of the heart is trouble,
And it always comes with the years,
And the smile that is worth the praises of earth
Is the smile that shines through tears.[7]

In the process of daily life, it is normal to experience highs and lows. President Boyd K. Packer says, "It is normal and healthy to be depressed occasionally."[8] Down cycles are part of the natural opposition of life. When President Packer hears a missionary say, "I have had just a miserable day. Everything has gone wrong, and I am discouraged. It just isn't going to go right. I feel very depressed," he answers, "Well, I am glad to hear that. At least I know you are normal! Did you know that it is not either normal or healthy to be on cloud nine all the time?"

He enjoys quoting this poem, a counterpoint to the poem I just shared:

Life is full of problems,
It's full of ifs and buts,
And the man that's grinning all the time
Must be completely nuts.[9]

Life's challenges bring out the best or the worst in us. When a driver cuts us off in traffic, we face a choice to get angry or to show restraint. It is important to affirm that no one makes us angry—that is a choice, an exercise of our moral agency. The split second when we choose our reaction is the surest proof of our character. But when we make mistakes, let's not turn into Eeyore. You remember Eeyore from *Winnie the Pooh*. He walked around moping and feeling that nothing good would ever happen when, in fact, it often did. No amount of talking seemed to cheer him up because he wanted to believe the worst about each situation. Instead of moping around like Eeyore, let's embrace life like Tigger. Maybe Tigger was not the smartest, the steadiest, or the wisest, but he was a lot more fun to be around.

Living in the Present

When life knocks you down, don't sit in a puddle and pout. Get on your feet and wipe yourself off! God doesn't want us moping about the past or fretting about the future. In a BYU devotional, Elder Jeffrey R. Holland pleaded that we not

> dwell on days now gone, nor . . . yearn vainly for yesterdays, however good those yesterdays may have been. The past is to be learned from but not lived in. We look back to claim the embers from glowing experiences but not the ashes. And when we have learned what we need to learn and have brought with us the best that we have experienced, then we look ahead, we remember that faith is always pointed toward the future. Faith always has to do with blessings and truths and events that will yet be efficacious in our lives.[10]

I love the story of one old man who always seemed contented with life. Neighbors wondered what his secret was. He was not particularly wealthy. He was not all that healthy. Having no family nearby, he spent much of his day alone. But he expressed genuine interest in all around him, and he seemed to relish each new day.

When a young boy asked him why he was so happy, the man replied that it was because he had the precious present. The boy wondered what the present could be—could it be a bicycle? Some other great toy? He wished he could have the same gift and spent years worrying about how to get it.

The boy grew to manhood and continued searching for this secret to happiness. Over the years, the old man offered clues to help the boy discover what he meant: "The present has nothing to do with wishing. . . . When you have the present you will be perfectly content to be where you are. . . . The present is not something that someone gives you. . . . It is something that you give to yourself."[11]

Then one day it dawned on him what the old man had meant. The precious present was just that—the present, the here and now. It was not worrying about the past or fretting about the future, but living with gratitude in the present.

His first thought was to worry about the years he had spent looking for this present. Then he realized, with a start, that he had already slipped back into his old habit of worrying. As the years went on, he found great joy in his life's journey by living in the present. Perhaps that is what Ludwig Wittgenstein meant when he said, "He who lives in the present lives in eternity."[12] It seems that God somehow lives this way, for He says, "All things are present with me" (Moses 1:6).

The Miracle of a New Day

"Men are, that they might have joy" (2 Nephi 2:25). A key element of experiencing joy is showing gratitude to God for sustaining life from day to day. Until we lose a loved one, we often take for granted the miracle of continuing life. It is only through God's sustaining influence that we live and breathe from day to day.

Consider the miracle of sunlight, a power that vitalizes and sustains life. "Have you ever thought about the amount of light and energy generated by our sun?" asked Elder Joseph B. Wirthlin. "The amount is almost beyond comprehension. Yet the heat and light that we receive come as a free gift from God. This is another proof of the goodness of our Heavenly Father. The light from the sun breaks through space, bathing our planet as it encircles the sun with life-giving warmth and light. Without the sun, there could be no life on this planet; it would be forever barren, cold, and dark."[13]

Each morning, the dawn brings endless possibilities and challenges. Our family placed this quote on our bathroom mirrors:

> Each day is a lifetime in miniature. To awaken each morning is to be born again, to fall asleep at night is to die to the day. In between waking and sleeping are the golden hours of the day. What we cannot do for a lifetime we can do for a daytime. "Anyone," wrote Robert Louis Stevenson, "can live sweetly, patiently, lovingly, purely, till the sun goes down." Anyone can hold his temper for a day and guard the words he speaks. Anyone can carry his burden heroically for one day. Anyone can strive to be happy for a day and to spread happiness around. Anyone can radiate love for a day. . . . The supreme art of living is to strive to live each day well.[14]

I believe the art of living involves an act of spiritual creation, kneeling before our Maker and invoking divine help in the choices of the day. The art of living involves choosing faith over fear—accepting the challenges of the day with confidence that God will help us to meet those challenges. The art of living includes studying the scriptures (God's instruction books) and following the quiet promptings of the Holy Ghost. And the art of living involves showing gratitude (see Alma 34:38).

The Daily Practice of Gratitude

Gratitude is both a spontaneous reaction and a learned behavior that can be developed and practiced over time. One young mother learned gratitude from her three-year-old son's prayers. One night by his bedside, he prayed, "I'm thankful for Mommy and Daddy, snow and clouds. I'm thankful for Santa Claus. I'm thankful for pizza and my big brother. Thank you for food. Thank you for everything." Then he finished emphatically with, "Oh, and please bless our dumb old cat." This mother wrote: "How much he had packed into his prayer! If only my prayers were so sincere. If only my heart were filled with such gratitude for simple aspects of everyday life. I liked to think I omitted such items because they were too insignificant to include among important adult acknowledgments and appeals. But I knew that in reality I no longer noticed them. I had become so entrenched in 'to do' lists and responsibilities that I no longer paid attention to the tiny purple flowers dotting the backyard, the intricacies of leaves, or the earth-washed smell of fresh rain. If I wasn't even aware of these pleasures, how could I be thankful for them?"

The decision to be grateful is a process—like practicing the piano. As we practice gratitude, we begin to notice daily miracles. This young mother reflected: "I began to see sunsets. Had they always been there? I started to haul my family outside to watch the sky's extraordinary hues of purple and pink. I began to see the beauty in my baby's face—even when it was covered with mashed green peas and congealed chicken gravy. I watched my husband tenderly tuck our sons into their beds at night and remembered how much I loved him. . . . I'd always thought gratitude was a feeling like love or anger—something that came naturally. But gratitude is more a virtue, like hope or faith—something that may not come naturally but can be learned (or relearned) by becoming as little children."[15]

The Lord warns us, "In nothing doth man offend God, or against none is his wrath kindled, save those who confess not his hand in all things, and obey not his commandments" (D&C 59:21). When we overlook the blessings He sends us, we are like selfish children, feeling sorry for ourselves because we do not have it all. We are so wrapped up in our own needs that we are not growing spiritually.

To put the need for gratitude into perspective, consider the experience of a parent who has scraped and saved every penny to buy Christmas gifts, only to have the children grumble and complain. The gifts are good, but the children covet that one "special gift" that cost too much or was unavailable. Of course, it is human nature to want more, but this natural selfishness hurts the feelings of a parent who has sacrificed much to make his or her children happy. I believe our Father in Heaven, who has sacrificed more than all of us, grieves when we overlook His daily bounteous blessings. In the daily press of life, we often forget to return thanks for the blessings of the day. After all, nine of the ten lepers did not return to thank the Master. If 90 percent of the people are ungrateful, how does that make our Father in Heaven feel?

But it's not just about how He feels; it's also about how we feel when we are grateful. God wants us to be grateful because when we acknowledge His hand in all things, our spirits are humble and contrite, teachable, and pliable. "It's pretty hard, if not impossible, to say 'Woe is me' at the same time you are saying, 'How blessed I am.' "[16] Martin Seligman, the father of positive psychology, has run clinical tests on many solutions for discouragement over the years. He found that one of the best ways to help someone who is struggling is to have them write down, before they go to bed each night, three things that went well that day. Simple? Yes. Effective? Absolutely.

I believe a prayer of gratitude is also a key to happiness. "O how you ought to thank your heavenly King!" King Benjamin teaches. "If you should render all the thanks and praise which your whole soul has power to possess, to that God who has created you, and has kept and preserved you . . . and is preserving you from day to day, by lending you breath, . . . yet ye would be unprofitable servants" (Mosiah 2:19–21).

Have you ever offered a prayer consisting only of thanks? What a blessing it is to do so! God has wrought so many miracles that we forget about daily. Elder Bruce R. McConkie urged us to "live in thanksgiving daily," showing our gratitude for God through prayer, through song, and especially through the way we live. Our list of things to be thankful for could include the beauties of the Creation, the mere fact of our existence, and the Atonement of Christ, which frees us from death and makes eternal life possible for the faithful. Our list could include the restored gospel of Jesus Christ and the scriptures, temples and sealing ordinances that allow us to live together forever as eternal families, and inspired prophets who lead and direct the Church. Our list might also include the freedoms we enjoy, such as the right to worship God according to the dictates of our own conscience. In short, Elder McConkie said that we should be thankful for "all the good things of life."[17]

I believe when we show gratitude for the gifts God showers upon us each day, we live in thanksgiving daily—no matter what season the calendar says it is. May we choose to be of good cheer despite the challenges we face. And may we become as little children and feel the hope and magic of a new day, remembering to thank the giver of the gift.

NOTES

1. Henry B. Eyring, "O Remember, Remember," *Ensign*, Nov. 2007, 67.

2. Amanda Dickson, *Wake Up to a Happier Life: Finding Joy in the Work You Do Every Day* (Salt Lake City: Shadow Mountain, 2007), 71.

3. Ibid., 91.

4. Jeffrey R. Holland, "The Tongue of Angels," *Ensign*, May 2007, 17.

5. Orson F. Whitney, in Conference Report, Apr. 1917, 43.

6. Quoted in Sheri L. Dew, *Go Forward with Faith: The Biography of Gordon B. Hinckley* (Salt Lake City: Deseret Book, 1996), 423.

7. Ella Wheeler Wilcox, "Worth While," in *Best-Loved Poems of the LDS People*, ed. Jack M. Lyon and others (Salt Lake City: Deseret Book, 2008), 7.

8. Boyd K. Packer, *Mine Errand from the Lord: Selections from the Sermons and Writings of Boyd K. Packer* (Salt Lake City: Deseret Book, 2008), 7.

9. Ibid., 530.

10. Jeffrey R. Holland, "Remember Lot's Wife," BYU devotional, January 13, 2009.

11. Adapted from Spencer Johnson, *The Precious Present* (New York: Doubleday, 1984).

12. Quoted in *The Book of Positive Quotations*, comp. John Cook (Minneapolis: Fairview Press, 1993), 227.

13. Joseph B. Wirthlin, "The Unspeakable Gift," *Ensign*, May 2003, 26.

14. Wilferd A. Peterson, www.livinglifefully.com/journeys/journey9.htm.

15. Lisa Ray Turner, "The Song of Gratitude," *Ensign*, July 1992, 51–52.

16. Brent L. Top, *When You Can't Do It Alone* (Salt Lake City: Deseret Book, 2008), 43.

17. Bruce R. McConkie, *Mormon Doctrine*, 2nd ed. (Salt Lake City: Deseret Book, 1979), 788.

2. The Gift of the *Plan*

"O how great the plan of our God!"
—2 Nephi 9:13

Latter-day Saint funerals are remarkable experiences. On the one hand, we solemnly mourn the passing of a loved one. But, on the other, we celebrate his life, considering his passing as a kind of graduation ceremony from mortality. With an eye of faith, we imagine the person parting the veil of eternity to return to his heavenly home. In fact, we may secretly envy him for successfully passing through the veil, as one patriarch stated, "*safely dead with [his] testimony burning brightly.*"[1] This eternal perspective comes from our Father in Heaven, who has revealed the plan of salvation, including the truth that death is not the end but the doorway to a new existence.

A Way Back

In the plan of salvation, we can compare life to a path leading back to our Heavenly Father. As we journey back to Him, we need a road map—or, better yet, a navigation system. As with any path, there will be easy parts, hard parts, and the occasional bumps and bruises. There is even danger in falling off the path.

President Spencer W. Kimball said, "The road of life is plainly marked according to the divine purpose, the map of the gospel of Jesus Christ is made available to the travelers, the destination of eternal life is clearly established. At that destination our Father waits hopefully, anxious to greet his returning children. Unfortunately, many will not arrive."[2]

When my daughter and I went to California for a winter break, we rented a car with a navigation system that guided us through the tangled web of the California highway system. I nicknamed it "HAL" after the computer in *2001: A Space Odyssey.* A few times I would punch in the destination and exit the parking lot, only to find I was heading the wrong way. Fortunately, the computer sensed my plight immediately and said, "Recalculating route, you dummy." He would then give me new directions to get back on course. My detours cost me time, but we were always able to get to our destination. Likewise, the Holy Ghost is our guide to help us stay on the right road or get back on track when we take a wrong turn. Probably more than a few times, the Holy Ghost wants to tell me, "Recalculating route, you dummy." Somehow He shows remarkable restraint.

The Council in Heaven

Through the Prophet Joseph Smith, the Lord revealed things hidden from before the foundation of the world. He taught that before our birth, we lived as spirits with Heavenly Father and our Elder Brother, Jesus Christ. There we received our first lessons in obedience, faith, and repentance. The Father then called a great council in heaven and spoke boldly of a plan to create an earth for us to dwell on.

In our premortal home, Heavenly Father essentially told us, "Now, my beloved children, in your spirit state you have progressed about as far as you can. To continue your development, you need physical bodies. I intend to provide a plan whereby you may continue your growth. As you know, one can grow only by overcoming."[3] Leaving the presence of our heavenly parents, we could more fully develop self-discipline and practice obeying His commandments (see Abraham 3:22–25). Much like our own mortal childhood, we were nurtured constantly at first and then gradually grew up to accept more responsibility, and finally moved out on our own—at least ideally!

As children of God, we believe our Father sent us to earth not to fail but to succeed. We believed He would guide us homeward, sending us parents, prophets, and Church leaders to teach His commandments and help us become a little more like Him day by day. A beloved hymn testifies of these truths:

> I am a child of God,
> And he has sent me here
> Has given me an earthly home
> With parents kind and dear.
>
> Lead me, guide me, walk beside me,
> Help me find the way.
> Teach me all that I must do
> To live with him someday.[4]

With all the tender regard of a loving parent, God knew that as toddlers, we would take our first faltering steps but often fall down and scrape our knees. Because He could not be with us, He entrusted us to the care of earthly parents who would nurture us to adulthood (and learn a lot about themselves in the process). And with the wisdom of an all-knowing being, He allows us to learn from our mistakes, our wise choices, our triumphs, and our tragedies.

Memories Veiled at Birth

Because the memory of our premortal home would be veiled, we would need to rely on Jesus Christ and His prophets and learn to obey the commandments using the precious gift of agency. We would need to follow the Savior with faith in His ability to save us, repenting of our sins when we made poor choices. In the premortal life, we knew that we had to accept baptism by immersion for the remission of sins and then renew that covenant through worthily partaking of the sacrament. We knew that the gift of the Holy Ghost would be an essential guide on our journey home. And we knew that being sealed by sacred priesthood power was an essential step toward eternal life. The poet Eliza R. Snow wrote,

> For a wise and glorious purpose
> Thou hast placed me here on earth
> And withheld the recollection
> Of my former friends and birth;
> Yet oft-times a secret something
> Whispered, "You're a stranger here,"
> And I felt that I had wandered
> From a more exalted sphere.[5]

"While we lack recollection of our pre-mortal life," said President Kimball, "before coming to this earth all of us understood

definitely the purpose of our being here. We would be expected
to gain knowledge, educate ourselves, train ourselves. We were to
control our urges and desires, master and control our passions, and
overcome our weaknesses, small and large."[6] We rejoiced in this
opportunity.

The Bible gives us a glimpse into this sacred scene when the
Lord asked Job, "Where wast thou when I laid the foundations of the
earth? . . . When the morning stars sang together, and all the sons of
God shouted for joy" (Job 38:4, 7). Now that we are on earth, we
sometimes wonder what all the shouting was about.

"We understood well before we came to this vale of tears," said
President Kimball,

> that there would be sorrows, disappointments, hard work,
> blood, sweat, and tears, but in spite of all, we looked down and
> saw this earth being made ready for us, and we said in effect,
> "Yes, Father, in spite of all those things I can see great blessings
> that could come to me as one of thy sons or daughters; in
> taking a body I can see that I will eventually become immortal
> like thee, that I might overcome the effects of sin and be
> perfected, and so I am anxious to go to the earth at the first
> opportunity."[7]

The Gift of Agency

Though all of us would sometimes make poor choices, we understood that the Lord would honor our freedom to choose. The prin-
ciple of agency is so important that President David O. McKay wrote,
"Next to the bestowal of life itself, the right to direct that life is
God's greatest gift to man."[8] We are free to choose among an infinite

number of choices, but our fundamental choice can be simplified to two great options.

Option 1: "liberty and eternal life, through the great Mediator of all men" (2 Nephi 2:27). If we choose this option, we will still have to overcome trials, but we will gradually become as happy as He is.

Option 2: "captivity and death, according to the captivity and power of the devil" (v. 27). If we choose this option, we will face even greater trials as a consequence of our choices.

Maybe I am going out on a limb, but if we really considered the consequences, we would always choose the first option. The problem is that Option 1 takes more work. Thus, it is the road less taken because it requires us to climb against the natural forces of gravity, if you will. Of course, as anyone who has made a challenging climb can say, the experience is well worth the effort. I think of the path to Angels Landing in Zion National Park—a difficult hike, absolutely terrifying at times, but the view from the top is unbelievably beautiful.

A Savior Provided

Our Father knew that by granting us the gift of agency, we would naturally make many mistakes as we navigated our way back home. Jesus Christ, the Father's Beloved Son from the beginning, volunteered to pay the penalty for our sins, saying, "Father, thy will be done, and the glory be thine forever" (Moses 4:2). This attitude of putting the Father's will before His own characterized His earthly ministry. But even more important, Jesus put the welfare of His younger brothers and sisters before His own needs, ransoming us from our mistakes through the infinite Atonement.

Lucifer then brashly proposed an easier (albeit impossible) alternative: "Behold, here am I, send me, I will be thy son, and I will redeem all mankind, that one soul shall not be lost." This proposal surely appealed to those who wanted a free ride to exaltation, a 100 percent guarantee that all would be saved. Then Lucifer added in what must have been an affront to the Father: "Surely *I* will do it; wherefore give *me* thine honor" (Moses 4:1; emphasis added). What an outrage! Lucifer essentially wanted to do the impossible: make people perfect without having them learn from their mistakes, and, in the process, take his father's honor.

Of course, the Father chose Jesus, His Well-Beloved from the beginning. Eliza R. Snow penned her gratitude for the Council in Heaven:

> How great the wisdom and the love
> That filled the courts on high
> And sent the Savior from above
> To suffer, bleed, and die! . . .
> He marked the path and led the way,
> And ev'ry point defines
> To light and life and endless day
> Where God's full presence shines.[9]

The majority of us understood that we would make mistakes, but that we would grow as we exercised agency. We would learn from earth life, experiencing "suffering, pain, sorrow, temptation and affliction, as well as the pleasures of life."[10] If we proved faithful in keeping His commandments, "we would be like him, and would have glorious bodies shining like the sun, as his glorious body shines, and should be clothed with the fulness of all the blessings of his kingdom."[11]

Unfortunately, not all of us rejoiced in the Father's choice. Led by Lucifer, one-third of the spirit children of our Father in Heaven turned against His plan (see D&C 29:36). Apparently, they wanted a free ride through mortality, as promised by the father of lies. Think how easy it would be to reap the reward without doing any hard work.

Elder Bruce C. Hafen once described a brand-new music school with an innovative approach to learning music—the "think method." The school's slogan was "Learn to play the piano without practicing."

In this innovative approach, students listened as their teacher talked about great music and shared passages from the best books. They talked in great detail about how to move their fingers over the keyboard.

After studying for years, the students could close their eyes and see the music flowing in front of them. They could tell you everything about it.

Finally, the students gathered to offer a recital. The first graduate of the "Do It without Practice Piano Course" walked onto the stage of Carnegie Hall with the orchestra in the background. What do you think happened?

Of course, not much.

"Why?" asked Elder Hafen. It is because "some things can be learned only by practice."[12] Life is like that too. We learn best by doing. Pure theory will not cut it—we have to put the theory into practice.

Choosing to follow the Master would require effort and exertion. But people grow stronger by overcoming resistance, as any weight lifter knows. I remember overhearing a conversation in the faculty weight room one day. "What are you going to do today?" the first professor asked.

"I'm going to lift weights," came the reply.

The first looked shocked, paused for dramatic effect, and then quipped, "Aren't those things heavy?"

Of course, the path of least resistance does not make us stronger. In fact, as BYU professor Joseph Fielding McConkie often said to his classes, "The pursuit of easy things makes men weak."

Tried and Tempted

After God cast out Satan and his followers, they tried to thwart God's plan of happiness by making us miserable like them. In mortality, Satan tries to lead us on a sort of spiritual snipe hunt, said Bishop Richard C. Edgley, distracting us and leading us away from our goal of eternal life.

"Among other things Satan would have us put in our bags," said Bishop Edgley, "is immorality in all its forms, including pornography, language, dress, and behavior. But such evil deeds bring emotional distress, loss of spirituality, loss of self-respect, and lost opportunity for a mission or temple marriage, and sometimes even unwanted pregnancy. Satan would enslave us by having us put drugs, alcohol, tobacco, and other addictive behaviors into our bags."[13]

It is a sad fact that those who wallow in worldliness are not content to do it alone but want to drag others down to their level. The message Satan blares from the loudspeakers of the world is, "Eat, drink, and be merry, for tomorrow we die" (2 Nephi 28:7). Unfortunately, many of the faithful, when taunted by their wayward siblings, fall into forbidden paths and become lost (see 1 Nephi 8:28).

We knew in mortality that we would be "tested by temptation, by trials, perhaps by tragedy," said President Packer. This knowledge helps us "to make sense of life and to resist the disease of doubt and despair and depression."[14]

The words of Elder Orson F. Whitney add this encouragement:

> No pain that we suffer, no trial that we experience is wasted. It ministers to our education, to the development of such qualities as patience, faith, fortitude and humility. All that we suffer and all that we endure, especially when we endure it patiently, builds up our characters, purifies our hearts, expands our souls, and makes us more tender and charitable, more worthy to be called the children of God, . . . and it is through sorrow and suffering, toil and tribulation, that we gain the education that we come here to acquire.[15]

As Latter-day Saints, we are grateful for the knowledge of the great plan of happiness and the central role of Jesus Christ in it. This eternal perspective gives us hope for the future, especially when we face the trials and temptations of mortal life. Because Christ returned to His Father, so can we. Because Christ overcame, so can we.

NOTES

1. Quoted in M. Russell Ballard, "The Greater Priesthood: Giving a Lifetime of Service in the Kingdom," *Ensign*, Sept. 1992, 73; emphasis added.

2. *Teachings of Presidents of the Church: Spencer W. Kimball* (Salt Lake City: The Church of Jesus Christ of Latter-day Saints, 2006), 8.

3. *Teachings of Presidents of the Church: Spencer W. Kimball*, 2.

4. Naomi Ward Randall, "I Am a Child of God," *Children's Songbook* (Salt Lake City: The Church of Jesus Christ of Latter-day Saints, 1989), 2–3.

5. Eliza R. Snow, "O My Father," *Hymns* (Salt Lake City: The Church of Jesus Christ of Latter-day Saints, 1985), no. 292.

6. *Teachings of Presidents of the Church: Spencer W. Kimball*, 3.

7. Ibid.

8. *Teachings of Presidents of the Church: David O. McKay* (Salt Lake City: The Church of Jesus Christ of Latter-day Saints, 2003), 208.

9. Eliza R. Snow, "How Great the Wisdom and the Love," *Hymns*, no. 195.

10. Joseph Fielding Smith, *Selections from Doctrines of Salvation* (Salt Lake City: The Church of Jesus Christ of Latter-day Saints, 2001), 45.

11. Ibid., 53.

12. Bruce C. Hafen, "The Value of the Veil," *Ensign*, June 1977, 11–12.

13. Richard C. Edgley, "Satan's Bag of Snipes," *Ensign*, Nov. 2000, 43.

14. Packer, *Mine Errand from the Lord*, 3.

15. Orson F. Whitney, quoted in *Improvement Era*, Mar. 1966, 211.

3. The Gift of *God's Son*

"For God so loved the world, that he gave his only begotten Son, that whosoever believeth in him should not perish, but have everlasting life."
—JOHN 3:16

Christians around the world gratefully acknowledge the matchless gift of God's Only Begotten Son. We rejoice that the Life and Light of the World descended from His throne divine to be born in humble circumstances in a stable in Bethlehem.

As the young Jesus learned lessons under the tutelage of Joseph and Mary, He increased in favor with God and man (Luke 2:52), growing to maturity until fully prepared to work His mortal ministry. I note with gratitude that He experienced all the challenges of mortality, becoming hungry, thirsty, and fatigued so that He might know how to succor us in our afflictions (see Mosiah 3:7).

Baptized in order to fulfill all righteousness, the Messiah received the gift of the Holy Ghost in its fullness and went about doing good by preaching the gospel, healing the sick and afflicted, and preparing His disciples to lead the Church after He was gone. When His mortal ministry reached its climax, He taught His disciples in the Upper Room, blessed and broke bread and offered wine as a symbol of His sacrifice, and then suffered for our sins in Gethsemane. Then on Golgotha, He cared for us enough to die for us. On the third day, He broke the bands of death, rising from the Garden Tomb and making the gift of Resurrection available for all.

Gethsemane

After Jesus completed His tutoring of the Apostles in the Upper Room, He took the disciples to the Garden of Gethsemane on the Mount of Olives, a place they frequently visited to pray and listen to their Master. We can picture the gnarled and twisted trunks of the olive trees in the moonlight, an image that suggests the suffering of the Savior for our sins.

Regarding this experience, President Joseph Fielding Smith wrote: "He carried, in some way that I cannot understand and you cannot understand, the burden of the combined sins of the world. It is hard enough for me to carry my own transgressions, and it is hard enough for you to carry yours. . . . I have seen [people] cry out in anguish because of their transgressions—just one individual's sins. Can you comprehend the suffering of Jesus when he carried, not merely by physical manifestation but in some spiritual and mental condition or manner, the combined weight of sin?"[1]

Under this tremendous weight of our sins and afflictions, our beloved Savior fell to the ground and prayed, saying, "Father, if thou be willing, remove this cup from me: nevertheless not my will, but thine, be done" (Luke 22:42). From unknown eons before the foundations of the earth were laid, the Firstborn Son had volunteered to become our Savior, saying, "Thy will be done, and the glory be thine forever" (Moses 4:2). Jesus had always put the Father before Himself, and the welfare of His siblings before His own. But now the awful weight of the combined sins and anguish of all mankind caused Him to shrink and wish that He might not partake of the bitter cup.

"Our finite mortal minds cannot grasp the tremendous load borne by the Savior in Gethsemane," wrote Andrew C. Skinner.

> But we begin to comprehend what this means in practical terms by remembering that this earth alone has had some 60 to 70 billion people live upon it during its temporal history. Each one of these 60 to 70 billion people has committed sin. . . . Multiply the sins, sorrows, heartaches, and injustices of these 60 to 70 billion souls by the millions of earths that the Savior created and redeemed, and we may begin to view the term "infinite atonement" in a different light.[2]

The glorious news of the gospel is that the Atonement is not only *infinite* but also *intimate* in its personal reach—all of us are within reach of God's love.

Stephen E. Robinson offered this perspective:

> All the negative aspects of human existence brought about by the Fall, Jesus Christ absorbed into himself. He experienced vicariously in Gethsemane all the private griefs and heartaches, all the physical pains and handicaps, all the emotional burdens and depressions of the human family. He knows the loneliness of those who don't fit in, or who aren't handsome or pretty. . . . He knows the anguish of parents whose children go wrong. He knows these things personally and intimately because he lived them in the Gethsemane experience. Having personally lived a perfect life, he then chose to experience our imperfect lives. In that infinite Gethsemane experience, in the meridian of time, the center of eternity, he lived a billion billion lifetimes of sin, pain, disease, and sorrow.[3]

Though Jesus was willing to bear our burdens from before the foundations of the world, the agony of that moment caused Him, "the greatest of all, to tremble because of pain, and to bleed at every pore" (D&C 19:18). The word *Gethsemane* means "olive press." In the garden, olives were pressed under a great stone wheel to release their precious oil, which initially comes out a blood-red color, then later turns clear. In a similar manner, our Savior "was literally pressed under the weight of the sins of the world," wrote Elder Russell M. Nelson. "He sweated great drops of blood—his life's 'oil'—which issued from every pore."[4] Today when we are anointed with consecrated oil, we remember the symbolism of the oil press of Gethsemane.

Elder Orson F. Whitney shared a dream he had of Gethsemane:

> I seemed to be in the Garden of Gethsemane, a witness of the Savior's agony. I saw Him as plainly as ever I have seen anyone. Standing behind a tree in the foreground, I beheld Jesus, with Peter, James and John, as they came through a little wicket gate at my right. Leaving the three Apostles there, after telling them to kneel and pray, the Son of God passed over to the other side, where He also knelt and prayed. It was the same prayer with which all Bible readers are familiar: "Oh my Father, if it be possible, let this cup pass from me; nevertheless not as I will, but as thou wilt."
>
> As He prayed the tears streamed down his face, which was toward me. I was so moved at the sight that I also wept, out of pure sympathy. My whole heart went out to him; I loved him with all my soul, and longed to be with him as I longed for nothing else.
>
> Presently He arose and walked to where those Apostles were kneeling—fast asleep! He shook them gently, awoke them, and

in a tone of tender reproach, untinctured by the least show of anger or impatience, asked them plaintively if they could not watch with him one hour. There He was, with the awful weight of the world's sin upon his shoulders, with the pangs of every man, woman and child shooting through his sensitive soul—and they could not watch with him one poor hour![5]

Applying this to our own lives, may we never fall asleep at our post but serve faithfully always.

As Christ suffered, the Father sent an angel to comfort and strengthen Him in His hour of need (see Luke 22:43). If heaven offered help for the Savior of the world in His hour of need, surely mercy is available for us, who are much weaker. In this light, Elder Jeffrey R. Holland said,

> I testify of angels, both the heavenly and the mortal kind. In doing so I am testifying that God never leaves us alone, never leaves us unaided in the challenges that we face. "[N]or will he, so long as time shall last, or the earth shall stand, or there shall be one man [or woman or child] upon the face thereof to be saved." On occasions, global or personal, we may feel we are distanced from God, shut out from heaven, lost, alone in dark and dreary places. Often enough that distress can be of our own making, but even then the Father of us all is watching and assisting. And always there are those angels who come and go all around us, seen and unseen, known and unknown, mortal and immortal.[6]

After the Savior finished praying the third time, He woke the Apostles, saying that the betrayer was on his way. Judas shortly appeared to betray our Lord for thirty pieces of silver.

Golgotha

Late that night and into the next day, our Lord and Savior was accused by Annas and Caiaphas, arraigned before Pilate, mocked by Herod, and finally sentenced to die at Golgotha, the place of burial.

President Kimball wrote movingly of the Savior's patience: "He who created the world and all that is in it, he who made the silver from which the pieces were stamped which bought him, he who could command defenders on both sides of the veil—stood and suffered."

Then he added:

> Unworthy men lashed him, the pure and the Holy One, the Son of God. One word from his lips and all his enemies would have fallen to the earth, helpless. All would have perished, all could have been as dust and ashes. Yet, in calmness, he suffered. . . .
>
> How he must have suffered when they violated his privacy by stripping off his clothes and then putting on him the scarlet robe!
>
> Then, the crown of thorns. How painful and excruciating! And yet, such equanimity! Such strength! Such control! It is beyond imagination.[7]

Soldiers forced Jesus in His drained and weakened condition to carry the cross, the instrument of His death. On the hill of Golgotha, they pounded nails into His hands and feet, and then, fearing that the weight of His body would be too heavy, they pounded nails into His wrists as well.

To imagine the Savior hanging on the cross is almost too painful to visualize, but this is one of the most important things we can do as we partake of the sacrament. Each week when we partake of the

Bread of Life, we remember His body, which was broken for us. Each week when we partake of the Living Water, we remember His blood, which was shed for us.

The eternal message of the Atonement is that He cared for us enough to die for us:

> I stand all amazed at the love Jesus offers me,
> Confused at the grace that so fully he proffers me.
> I tremble to know that for me he was crucified,
> That for me, a sinner, he suffered, he bled and died. . . .
>
> I think of his hands pierced and bleeding to pay the debt!
> Such mercy, such love, and devotion can I forget?
> No, no, I will praise and adore at the mercy seat,
> Until at the glorified throne I kneel at his feet.
>
> Oh, it is wonderful that he should care for me
> Enough to die for me!
> Oh, it is wonderful, wonderful to me![8]

Even as Christ hung on the cross, He showed compassion to all those around Him. Regarding His oppressors, He cried, "Father, forgive them; for they know not what they do" (Luke 23:34). Later, in what is one of the most magnificent displays of love in all recorded scripture, the dying Christ invited John to care for Mary as his own mother (see John 19:26). There is perhaps no more moving testimony of His love and compassion as He looked to help others in the midst of the violence being done to Him.

While Jesus hung on the cross, He felt the agony of Gethsemane return. In Gethsemane, Christ drank from the bitter cup so that we might not have to, but Gethsemane "was not the end of the bitter cup.

At Golgotha the bitter cup was refilled and drunk again."[9] Overcome by grief, Jesus felt that the end was near. At this hour, He felt a final agony—the loss of His Father's companionship. We picture the Father in His courts on high, grieving for the death of His dearly beloved Son and finally turning away in anguish. Unlike the experience of Abraham and Isaac, this time there was no ram in the thicket. This time the sacrifice had to go on.

Feeling the loss of His Father's companionship, Jesus cried aloud, "My God, my God, why hast thou forsaken me?" (Matthew 27:46). At last, He prayed submissively, "Father, it is finished, thy will is done!" (JST, Matthew 27:54, footnote *a*).

These words place finality on His earlier prayer in Gethsemane. Now the Father's will had been done.

Having completed all He was sent on earth to do, Jesus then cried with a loud voice, "Father, into thy hands I commend my spirit" (Luke 23:46). Yielding up His life, our great high priest then parted the veil of eternity. There he entered the world of spirits and preached to the assembled multitude the joyous message of "the resurrection and the redemption of mankind from the fall, and from individual sins on conditions of repentance" (D&C 138:19). While His body was buried in the tomb of Joseph of Arimathea, His spirit continued to be about His Father's business. In the spirit world, Christ organized His great missionary force to preach the good news of the gospel to the wicked and disobedient, fulfilling the prophecy that the Messiah would "proclaim liberty to the captives, and the opening of the prison to them that are bound" (Isaiah 61:1; see D&C 138:18).

Garden Tomb

Jesus rose from the tomb on the third day, unlocking the gates of death and making resurrection possible for all mankind. This was the crowning moment of the Atonement. Jesus had opened for all of us the gateway to immortality and eternal life. No wonder all Christendom joins in singing the Easter hymn,

> He is risen! He is risen!
> Tell it out with joyful voice.
> He has burst his three days' prison;
> Let the whole wide earth rejoice.
> Death is conquered, man is free.
> Christ has won the victory.[10]

Just as death entered the world in the Garden of Eden, the Atonement was wrought in the Garden of Gethsemane, and the firstfruits of the Resurrection rose from the Garden Tomb. How appropriate it was that Mary Magdalene supposed that Jesus was a gardener, for these transcendent events had all been accomplished in gardens!

Trees are recurring themes in these locations: the tree of knowledge of good and evil in Eden, the olive trees in Gethsemane, the dead tree of the cross of Calvary, and ultimately the tree of life. These events are linked together in Christ.

> Long ago within a garden,
> Mother Eve ate of a tree.
> Death would be our awful burden;
> Only one could set us free.
>
> Humbly suff'ring in a garden,
> Kneeling near an olive tree,

Pressed beneath sin's awful burden,
Jesus prayed to set us free.

In a tomb within a garden,
People went to where He lay,
Angels told them, "He is risen,"
On that glorious Easter day.

Come to Christ and be forgiven,
Taste the fruit of Father's tree,
Sweetest fruit of all His garden,
Come to him and be set free.

Alleluia! Alleluia!
Jesus came to set us free.
Son of God and true Messiah,
Songs of joy we raise to thee.[11]

Accepting the Gift

At Easter, we celebrate the Atonement of Jesus Christ as "the great-est of all gifts."[12] Through the Atonement, Jesus made salvation free to all those who come unto Him and forsake their sins (a conditional gift). Through His death and Resurrection, Jesus freed all of us from the bonds of death (an unconditional gift). As Latter-day Saints, we rejoice in the Atonement as "the central fact, the crucial foundation, the chief doctrine, and the greatest expression of divine love in the plan of salvation."[13]

Though we rejoice in this glorious gift, sometimes we struggle because of our sins and lose hope because of our mortal failings. Sometimes we buy into Satan's lies that we are simply not cut out for heaven. "For some reason," wrote President Packer, "we think the

Atonement of Christ applies only at the end of mortal life to redemption from the Fall, from spiritual death. *It is much more than that.* It is an ever-present power to call upon in everyday life. When we are racked or harrowed up or tormented by guilt or burdened with grief, He can heal us."[14] This promise is true. The Savior is mighty enough, is capable enough to change our very natures and make us better than we are—if we will let Him. Through the marvelous power of the Creator, we can be transformed in Christ.

The Savior is truly on our side, understanding our temptations and afflictions and showering us with mercy when we repent. Jesus, who loved us from the beginning, pleads for us, saying, "Father, behold the sufferings and death of him who did no sin, in whom thou wast well pleased; behold the blood of thy Son which was shed, the blood of him whom thou gavest that thyself might be glorified; wherefore, Father, spare these my brethren that believe on my name, that they may come unto me and have everlasting life" (D&C 45:4–5). A beloved hymn proclaims:

> What a friend we have in Jesus,
> All our sins and griefs to bear! . . .
> O what peace we often forfeit,
> O what needless pain we bear,
> All because we do not carry
> Everything to God in prayer![15]

Indeed, what peace we often forfeit and what needless pain we bear when we try to shoulder the load alone! Jesus has carried the load for us, and He is willing to give us rest if we will take His yoke upon us (see Matthew 11:28).

The Parable of the Push-ups

The following story offers perspective on the Atonement, a matchless gift that some of us choose to reject:

A boy named Steve was struggling in school. He had been kicked out of several classes, but a kind seminary teacher finally allowed him into his sixth-period class. One day, the teacher planned a special lesson. He asked Steve to stay after class so he could talk with him. The teacher asked, "How many push-ups can you do?"

Steve replied, "I do about two hundred every night."

"Two hundred?" the teacher said. "That's pretty good. Do you think you could do three hundred?"

Steve answered, "I don't know—I've never done three hundred at a time."

The teacher said, "Can you do three hundred in sets of ten?"

"Well, I think I can," Steve answered. "Yeah, I can do it."

"Good! I need you to do this on Friday."

Well, Friday came, and Steve went to class early and sat in front. When class started, the teacher pulled out a big box of donuts. Now, these weren't the normal kinds of donuts. They were the big, extra-fancy kind, with cream centers and frosting swirls. Everyone was excited. It was Friday, the last class of the day, and they were going to get an early start on the weekend.

The teacher went to the first girl in the first row and asked, "Cynthia, do you want a donut?" Cynthia said yes.

He then turned to Steve and asked, "Would you do ten push-ups so that Cynthia can have a donut?"

Steve said, "Sure," and jumped down from his desk to do a quick ten. Then Steve sat again at his desk. The teacher put a donut on

Cynthia's desk, then went to the next student and asked, "Joe, do you want a donut?" Joe said yes.

The teacher asked, "Steve, would you do ten push-ups so Joe can have a donut?"

And so it went, down the first aisle, and down the second aisle, until they came to Scott, the captain of the football team and center of the basketball team. When the teacher asked, "Scott, do you want a donut?" his reply was, "Well, can I do my own push-ups?"

The teacher said, "No, Steve has to do them."

Scott replied, "Well, I don't want one then."

The teacher then turned to Steve and asked, "Would you do ten push-ups so Scott can have a donut he doesn't want?"

Steve started to do ten push-ups. Scott said, "Hey! I said I didn't want one!"

The teacher said, "Just leave it on the desk if you don't want it," and he put a donut on Scott's desk.

Now, by this time, Steve had begun to slow down a little. He just stayed on the floor between sets because it took too much effort to be getting up and down. Beads of perspiration formed on his brow. The teacher started down the third row. Now the students were beginning to get a little angry.

The teacher asked Jenny, "Do you want a donut?" Jenny said no.

Then the teacher asked, "Steve, would you do ten push-ups so Jenny can have a donut that she doesn't want?" Steve did ten, and Jenny got a donut.

By now the students were beginning to say no regularly, and there were many uneaten donuts on the desks. Steve was also really putting forth a lot of effort to get these push-ups done for each donut.

Sweat was dripping onto the floor beneath his face. His arms and face were red from the effort.

The teacher said he couldn't bear to watch all of Steve's work for those uneaten donuts, so he asked Robert to make sure Steve did the push-ups. The teacher started down the fourth row.

During his class, some students had wandered in and sat along the heaters on the sides of the room. When the teacher realized this, he did a quick count and saw thirty-four students in the room. He started to worry if Steve would be able to make it.

The teacher went on to the next person and the next and the next. Near the end of that row, Steve was really having a rough time. He was taking a lot more time to complete each set.

A student named Jason came to the door and was about to come in when all the students yelled, "No! Don't come in! Stay out!"

Jason didn't know what was going on. Steve looked up and said, "No, let him come in."

The teacher said, "You realize that if Jason comes in you will have to do ten push-ups for him."

Steve said, "Yes, let him come in."

The teacher said, "Okay, I'll let you get Jason's out of the way right now. Jason, do you want a donut?"

"Yes."

"Steve, will you do ten push-ups so that Jason can have a donut?" Steve did ten push-ups very slowly and with great effort. Jason, bewildered, was handed a donut and sat down.

The teacher finished the fourth row, then started among those seated on the heaters. Steve's arms were now shaking with each push-up in a struggle to lift himself against the force of gravity. Sweat was dropping off of his face, and by this time there was not a dry eye in the room.

The last two girls in the room were cheerleaders. The teacher went to Linda, the second to last, and asked, "Linda, do you want a donut?"

Linda said very sadly, "No, thank you."

The teacher said, "Steve, would you do ten push-ups so that Linda can have a donut she doesn't want?"

Grunting from the effort, Steve did ten very slow push-ups for Linda.

Then the teacher turned to the last girl. "Susan, do you want a donut?" Susan, with tears flowing down her face, asked, "Can I help him?"

The teacher, with tears of his own, said, "No, he has to do it alone. Steve, would you do ten push-ups so Susan can have a donut?"

As Steve very slowly finished his last push-up, with the understanding that he had accomplished all that was required of him, having done 350 push-ups, his arms buckled beneath him, and he fell to the floor.

The teacher turned to his class and said, "And so it was that our Savior, Jesus Christ, prayed, 'Father, into thy hands I commend my spirit.' With the understanding that Jesus had done everything that was required of Him, He collapsed on the cross and died—even for those that didn't want His gift. And just like some of us, many choose not to accept the gift that was provided for them."[16]

It is my prayer that we will accept with even greater gratitude the matchless gift given in Gethsemane, on Golgotha, and in the Garden Tomb. May we acknowledge the priceless gift of God's Only Begotten Son, who showed us the way back to God, who drank the bitter cup of the Atonement, and who rose from the dead so that we might experience the gift of the Resurrection.

NOTES

1. Joseph Fielding Smith, *Doctrines of Salvation*, 1:129–30; quoted in Andrew C. Skinner, *Golgotha* (Salt Lake City: Deseret Book, 2004), 8.

2. Andrew C. Skinner, *Gethsemane* (Salt Lake City: Deseret Book, 2002), 57.

3. Stephen E. Robinson, Religious Education prayer meeting, February 12, 1992.

4. Russell M. Nelson, "Why This Holy Land?" *Ensign*, Dec. 1989, 17–18.

5. Orson F. Whitney, *Through Memory's Halls: The Life Story of Orson F. Whitney* (Independence, MO: Zion's Printing and Publishing, 1930), 82–83.

6. Jeffrey R. Holland, "The Ministry of Angels," *Ensign*, Nov. 2008, 31.

7. Spencer W. Kimball, "Jesus of Nazareth," *Ensign*, Dec. 1980, 6–7.

8. Charles H. Gabriel, "I Stand All Amazed," *Hymns*, no. 193.

9. Skinner, *Golgotha*, 1.

10. Cecil Frances Alexander, "He Is Risen," *Hymns*, no. 199.

11. Poem by author, "Long Ago within a Garden."

12. Packer, *Mine Errand from the Lord*, 46.

13. Jeffrey R. Holland, in *Jesus Christ and His Gospel: Selections from the Encyclopedia of Mormonism* (Salt Lake City: Deseret Book, 1992), 23–24.

14. Boyd K. Packer, "The Touch of the Master's Hand," *Ensign*, May 2001, 23; emphasis added.

15. This hymn has the same tune as "Israel, Israel, God Is Calling." See Karen Lynn Davidson, *Our Latter-day Hymns: The Stories and the Messages* (Salt Lake City: Deseret Book, 1988), 37.

16. Adapted from http://byauthorunknown.blogspot.com/2008/12/parable-of-push-ups.html.

4. The Gift of the *Resurrection*

"For this is my work and my glory—to bring to pass the immortality and eternal life of man."
—Moses 1:39

L et me take you back in time to a terrible Friday in Jerusalem. The devoted disciples of Christ had watched as their promised Messiah was betrayed, interrogated, then mocked, tortured, and crucified.

"How could this have happened?" they must have wondered. "Will He truly rise again?" We may forgive their questioning, for no one had risen from the grave as a resurrected being.

On Sunday the disciples, and many of the women who followed Christ, gathered to discuss the rumors that had been circulating. Mary Magdalene, Salome, and others testified of seeing the empty tomb and hearing angels declare, "He is risen," but were these simply stories of hysterical women who wanted to believe Jesus was not dead?

Imagine the disciples' shock when Jesus suddenly appeared in their midst. They were terrified. Calming their fears, Jesus spoke reassuringly, "Peace be unto you. . . . Why are you troubled? and why do thoughts arise in your hearts? Behold my hands and my feet, that it is I myself: handle me, and see; for a spirit hath not flesh and bones" (Luke 24:36, 38–39).

Allowing them to thrust their hands into His hands, feet, and side, He gently reproved Thomas for his earlier disbelief. Then He asked for food, providing another witness that He was indeed flesh and bones and not a spirit.

This trial of their faith was over. The disciples now knew with new certainty that death was not the end but was the beginning of another glorious experience. The miracle of the Resurrection was real! Because Christ rose again, so would they—and so shall we.

A few years ago Elder Joseph B. Wirthlin compared the trial of the disciples' faith to the difficulties we all face:

> Each of us will have our own Fridays—those days when the universe itself seems shattered and the shards of our world lie littered about us in pieces. We all will experience those broken times when it seems we can never be put together again. We will all have our Fridays. But I testify to you in the name of the One who conquered death—Sunday will come. In the darkness of our sorrow, Sunday will come. No matter our desperation, no matter our grief, Sunday will come. In this life or the next, Sunday will come.[1]

Elder Wirthlin then shared his hope of seeing his parents embrace once again. He shared his hope that soon he would embrace his beloved wife, Elisa. Now, with Elder Wirthlin's passing, I affirm that his long-awaited reunion has occurred. Sunday did come for him.

A Personal Reflection

Those who have lost loved ones look forward to the time when they will embrace those loved ones once again. I would like to share a personal story. Ten years ago I became violently ill, vomiting most of the night. The next morning, exhausted from the ordeal, I stayed home from church. Later that day, my wife, Patty, received a phone call from the hospital that her mom was in the emergency room and that we should visit her right away.

When we arrived at the hospital, Patty's sister Debbi said that they were doing CPR on Nana. Nana was dead? How was that possible? She was in her seventies and had reasonably good health except for a heart condition called cardiomyopathy, an enlarged heart (we always said she had a big heart!). Apparently, she had gone to the hospital with the flu and then her heart had suddenly stopped.

At the hospital, Nana's body continued to breathe, an involuntary response that cruelly mimicked life. Patty asked the nurses several times, "Are you sure she is dead?" They assured her that she was really gone. Patty wept and knelt at her mother's bedside for what seemed like hours. Exhausted and dehydrated, I tried to keep the busy toddlers from tearing up the waiting room. It was definitely not the best day in the history of our family.

We began making plans for a funeral in Orem and one in her hometown of Boise. No money had been set aside for funeral arrangements, so Wendell and I, her sons-in-law, paid most of the costs. To save money, Richard, a friend of the family, offered to transport the body and casket in an enclosed pickup truck. David, Patty's brother, felt compelled to leave as early as possible, but they were delayed several hours and left late in the afternoon to make the six-hour drive to Boise.

That night the weather was ominous, and the roads icy. As Patty and I drove in our minivan, we received a phone call with unbelievably bad news. The truck—with the casket in the back—had hit black ice and rolled over. As the news unfolded, it got worse. When the truck rolled over, Richard, the driver, had broken his neck. David, my brother-in-law, and his wife had been cut and bruised and were shaken up. And, adding insult to injury, Nana's body had come out of the casket. Her temple clothes were muddy, and the casket was ruined.

Numb with grief and pain, we went to the hospital. That night was an awful blur. We offered what comfort we could to David and his wife. Richard, who had a halo screwed to his scalp, was concerned that he might never walk again. The life-flight helicopter was warming up to take Richard to Salt Lake City, where they could better treat his serious injury. Wendell and I asked the doctors for a moment to give him a priesthood blessing. They said to hurry.

In the blessing, Wendell stated that Richard would walk again and be able to return to those activities he loved to do, including hunting. As he pronounced those promises, I was praying with all the energy of my heart that Heavenly Father would honor that blessing.

We continued to Boise the next day. Meanwhile, the funeral directors in Twin Falls had cleaned up the body. We bought another casket with our family's limited funds. Ironically, because of the accident, Nana arrived late to her own funeral.

The speakers delivered beautiful messages of hope and inspiration, but as I sang "I Stand All Amazed," I remember feeling a bit forsaken by my Father in Heaven.

We returned home safely, and life went on.

In the months that followed, Patty and I struggled to figure out what had gone wrong. How could He have allowed such a tragedy to occur? Why did it have to happen to us? Was it just bad luck that all these miserable events had collided in a most unfortunate series of events?

Several years later, I reflected on those events in my journal, asking for faith: "I pray that our merciful Savior will heal my soul. I do know, as Job, that He lives. Though He slay me, yet will I trust in Him. I do know that He is much more patient and long-suffering and far-seeing than I am. I also know that He has been exceedingly patient with my struggling over the years. I choose to trust in Jesus Christ, the Lord and Master of all. Dear Father, please send thy holy peace. Help thou mine unbelief. Be still, my soul."

Tested by Trials

The night of the accident was a long, hard time that tested my faith to the core. For a number of years, I asked the question, "How does a loving Father in Heaven let something like this happen?"

The answer to my prayer came only recently. As I was reading the scriptures and pondering the situation for the first time in many months, the thought came, "Don't blame God for accidents or human mistakes." I realized that He did not cause the accident, but neither did He prevent it from occurring. We sometimes walk on a wire without a safety net, and we should not blame God for not catching us when we fall.

Of course, this small tragedy really is insignificant when compared to other acts of senseless violence. Others in history have suffered infinitely more because of man's inhumanity to man: slavery and the suffering of those who fought in the Civil War; Jews in the Holocaust; and blacks and the suffering of civil rights activists all come to mind.

Now, years later, I can see the hand of Providence in the healing that has since come. Richard, the driver, recovered from his broken neck and went back to those activities he once enjoyed, though he walked with a limp thereafter. David and his wife healed from their wounds, and David returned to Church activity after many years of absence.

Despite these blessings, spiritual healing has taken some time. Though the memory of these events has faded a bit, the reality is still there. Nana's sudden death and my wife's long, slow grief left us feeling forsaken. The storms of life had drenched us to the skin.

Storms of Life

In mortality, we often think that if we are righteous, we will be sheltered. After all, the scriptures promise that God will prosper the righteous. Wasn't I trying to build my home upon the Rock of our Redeemer? Why did it feel like the rain came down and washed me away?

Well, sometimes when it rains, it pours. We read that God sends His rain "on the just and on the unjust" (Matthew 5:45). That does not mean He loves His children any less. When the rain falls, He does not put up a magic umbrella to keep us from getting wet, and He certainly doesn't make it rain everywhere except on His "good children."

Consider the testimony of President Thomas S. Monson: "Though the storm clouds may gather, though the rains may pour down upon us, our knowledge of the gospel and our love of our Heavenly Father and of our Savior will comfort and sustain us and bring joy to our hearts as we walk uprightly and keep the commandments. There will be nothing in this world that can defeat us. . . . Fear not. Be of good cheer. The future is as bright as your faith."[2]

One of my favorite hymns is "Be Still, My Soul." In it, Katarina von Schlegel writes:

> Be still, my soul: The Lord is on thy side;
> With patience bear thy cross of grief or pain.
> Leave to thy God to order and provide;
> In ev'ry change he faithful will remain.
> Be still, my soul: Thy best, thy heav'nly Friend
> Thru thorny ways leads to a joyful end.[3]

What is that joyful end? It is the Resurrection, a gift offered to all mankind. "What is it that ye shall hope for?" the prophet Mormon asks. Then he answers his own question: "That ye shall have hope through the atonement of Christ and the power of his resurrection, to be raised unto life eternal" (Moroni 7:41).

I love the Book of Mormon's clear commentary on the physical nature of the Resurrection. "The soul shall be restored to the body," Alma says, "and the body to the soul; yea, and every limb and joint shall be restored to its body; yea, even a hair of the head shall not be lost; but all things shall be restored to their proper and *perfect frame*" (Alma 40:23; emphasis added).

President Joseph F. Smith testifies that in the Resurrection, our "sleeping dust [will] be restored unto its *perfect frame*, bone to bone, and the sinews and the flesh upon [us], the spirit and the body to be united never again to be divided, that [we] might receive a fulness of joy" (D&C 138:17; emphasis added).

Joy in the Morning

The Psalmist taught, "Weeping may endure for a night, but joy cometh in the morning" (Psalm 30:5). We hope to be raised up in the morning of the First Resurrection. Perhaps then we can ask Nana what it was like to be late to her own funeral. Even though rain clouds gather and drench us from time to time, we know that God hears our prayers and answers them in His own time and way. We also believe the scriptural promise that Christ will heal all wounds and wipe away all tears from our eyes (see Revelation 21:4).

I testify that the gift of the Resurrection offers us this hope and good cheer. As Elder Wirthlin said, "No matter our desperation, no matter our grief, Sunday will come. In the darkness of our sorrow, Sunday will come." I raise my voice with his in testifying that Sunday will come.

NOTES

1. Joseph B. Wirthlin, "Sunday Will Come," *Ensign*, Nov. 2006, 30.
2. Thomas S. Monson, "Be of Good Cheer," *Ensign*, May 2009, 92.
3. Katharina von Schlegel, "Be Still, My Soul," *Hymns*, no. 124.

5. The Gift of the *Holy Ghost*

*"This Comforter is the promise which I give unto you
of eternal life."*
—DOCTRINE AND COVENANTS 88:4

A good Christian woman who had been guided by the Holy Ghost several times in her life eventually participated in the missionary discussions and joined The Church of Jesus Christ of Latter-day Saints. After her baptism, she shared her experience of receiving the gift of the Holy Ghost. "I felt the influence of the Holy Ghost settle upon me with greater intensity than I had ever felt before," she said. "He was like an old friend who had guided me in the past but now had come to stay."[1] The Holy Ghost is truly an old friend who knows us and cares about our welfare, warning of danger and comforting us during hard times. His still, small voice whispers peace and comforts us during times of trial.

A Quiet Voice of Warning

The voice of the Spirit is so quiet that we may miss it if we are not paying attention. "We do not have the words (even the scriptures do not have words) which perfectly describe the Spirit," President Packer said. "The scriptures generally use the word voice, which does not exactly fit. These delicate, refined spiritual communications are not seen with our eyes, nor heard with our ears. And even though it is described as a voice, it is a voice that one feels, more than one hears."[2] In order to perceive the guidance of the Spirit, we need to remain worthy and steer clear of the distractions of the world. It is difficult to feel the Spirit when we are watching inappropriate movies, listening to worldly music, or disobeying the commandments. Those delicate impressions are easily overlooked unless we are living worthily and seeking to be in tune with the spirit of revelation.

President Wilford Woodruff received many warnings protecting him and his family from physical danger. On one occasion, he traveled to the home of a Brother Williams in the eastern United States, where he had been called to serve a mission. He reported:

> I drove my carriage one evening into the yard of Brother Williams. Brother Orson Hyde drove a wagon by the side of mine. I had my wife and children in the carriage. After I turned out my team and had my supper, I went to bed in the carriage. I had not been there but a few minutes when the Spirit said to me, "Get up and move that carriage." I told my wife I had to get up and move the carriage. She said, "What for?" I said, "I don't know." That is all she asked me on such occasions; when I told her I did not know, that was enough. I got up and moved my carriage. . . . I then looked around me and went to bed. The same Spirit said, "Go and move your animals from that oak tree." . . . I went and moved my horses and put them in a little hickory grove. I again went to bed.
>
> In thirty minutes a whirlwind came up and broke that oak tree off within two feet from the ground. It swept over three or four fences and fell square in that dooryard, near Brother Orson Hyde's wagon, and right where mine had stood. What would have been the consequences if I had not listened to that

Spirit? Why, myself and wife and children doubtless would have been killed. That was the still, small voice to me—no earthquake, no thunder, no lightning; but the still, small voice of the Spirit of God. It saved my life. It was the spirit of revelation to me.[3]

"Go Check the Mail!"

The Spirit continues to warn us today. My friend Barbara shared a frightening experience she had while staying in her uncle and aunt's house in Los Angeles one summer. One weekend after her aunt had left home for a visit, Barbara drove up to the house and saw the garage door open. Thinking her aunt had forgotten to close it, she drove in, then walked into her bedroom. She was surprised to see her suitcase open on the bed and her dresser drawers open and thought her aunt must have been searching for something.

As she walked down the hallway, she grasped the handle of the bathroom door when a quiet voice inside her mind whispered, "Go check the mail!" The thought seemed very random, but she changed her course and walked out to check the mailbox outside. As she started back toward the house, she saw the hallway light turn off and realized someone was in the house. Heart pounding, she dropped the mail in the driveway and ran for help at a neighbor's house.

She writes,

> Twenty minutes later, I was numbly walking with two policemen through the upper floors of my uncle's ransacked, burglarized house. Couches were overturned, drawers were pulled out onto the floor, a stereo system and other valuables were missing. When we came to the bottom floor, I nearly fell

over when I saw my bedroom closet door and my bathroom door, both of which I had left closed, standing wide open. At least one burglar had been hiding behind each door! It wasn't until then that I fully understood the grave danger I had been in. That night, I fervently thanked my Heavenly Father that I had been prompted to turn away from the bathroom door.

Later I reflected on my patriarchal blessing, which urges me to always follow the promptings of the Spirit of the Holy Ghost. One promise of my blessing stood out in particular: If I would promptly do the things the Holy Ghost would place in my mind, I would be protected from crippling harm or injury.

How grateful I am for that quiet voice which whispered, "Go check the mail!" What a real and powerful influence the Holy Ghost can be. [Then she adds,] Although I will always remember how I was protected from possible physical harm that day, I am most grateful for the great spiritual protection and guidance the Holy Ghost has given me throughout my life.[4]

That spiritual guidance can help us navigate through the minefield of life, guiding us safely through trouble we may not even realize is all around us.

"Couldn't You Hear Me?"

As a fifteen-year-old teacher in the Aaronic Priesthood, I had an experience with the Spirit that profoundly affected me. While reading in my basement bedroom, I thought I heard someone call my name. It was so faint that I went upstairs to ask Mom if she had called me. She said she had not.

I still felt unsettled. I was positive that someone had called my name. I went back downstairs and began to read again but felt so uneasy that I decided to take another look around.

I opened the front door. No one was there. But I saw something unusual: the front door of our van was ajar. So I walked over to close it. To my shock, I saw my father's body lying face down in the snow with his leg caught in the door of the van. I thought he was dead.

In a raspy whisper, he said, "Couldn't you hear me? I've been calling for you."

He explained how an old back injury had flared up and how he had gone into back spasms just as he pulled up in the driveway. Trying to get out the van, he had fallen face-down into the snow with his leg trapped in the van. Suffering intense back spasms, he was unable to free his leg or signal us for help.

After my mom and I assisted him to his bed, it dawned on me that it would be highly unlikely for me to have heard his hoarse voice calling my name and that I had felt so unsettled as to search all over for the source of the sound. I concluded that the Holy Ghost was the source of the guidance that led me to seek out my dad.

I wonder if sometimes our lives are too noisy to hear the quiet whisper of the Spirit speaking to us. In those times, perhaps the Spirit would say the same thing my dad did: "Couldn't you hear me? I've been calling for you."

Peace in Times of Trial

The Holy Ghost is not only a warning voice but also a comforting influence in time of trouble. As Jesus introduced the ordinance of the sacrament, He told His disciples that they would receive the Holy

Ghost to teach them and to comfort them: "The Comforter, which is the Holy Ghost, whom the Father will send in my name, he shall teach you all things, and bring all things to your remembrance, whatsoever I have said unto you" (John 14:26). In the sacrament prayer, we are promised to have His Spirit to be with us as we remember the Savior and keep His commandments.

Jesus then prepared His disciples for the trials just ahead: "Peace I leave with you, my peace I give unto you: not as the world giveth, give I unto you. Let not your heart be troubled, neither let it be afraid" (John 14:27). Those blessings of peace are available for us today in our own hour of need.

In a moving Easter talk, former Relief Society general president Bonnie D. Parkin told how, as a child, she came to love her aunt Rachel through her mother's efforts to keep her memory alive. Aunt Rachel had died years earlier in a swimming accident, but her mother would share stories and tangible reminders. For example, her mother would talk about how close they used to be and all the fun things they did together. When the children were sick, her mother would wrap her up in an afghan her aunt had made, saying, "Let's put Aunt Rachel's arms around you." Though Aunt Rachel was far away, she seemed right next to her as the afghan was wrapped around her. In like manner, we feel the Savior's touch as we are wrapped in the warmth of the Comforter. We keep His presence close as we remember Him always. Sister Parkin says, "In my hours of need, my times of sickness, my discouragements and disappointments, I have felt his arms around me, wrapping me in everlasting love."[5]

We recognize the influence of the Spirit by the peace we feel. After the death of Joseph Smith, Brigham Young was struggling with how to lead the Church. In a dream, the Prophet Joseph Smith offered this counsel:

> Be careful and not turn away the small, still voice; it will teach them what to do and where to go; it will yield the fruits of the kingdom. Tell the brethren to keep their heart open to conviction, so that when the Holy Ghost comes to them their hearts will be ready to receive it. They can tell the Spirit of the Lord from all other spirits—it will whisper peace and joy to their souls; it will take malice, hatred, strife and all evil from their hearts, and their whole desire will be to do good.[6]

A Sanctifying Influence

The Holy Ghost is symbolically represented by fire, which can be either comforting (like a campfire) or purifying (like the refiner's fire). The gift of the Holy Ghost is called the baptism by fire because of the way it purifies us. As we continue to repent and follow the guidance of the Holy Ghost, we are sanctified through the Spirit and enabled to return to our Father's presence. Sometimes that sanctification comes during times of deep distress, as it did for the Prophet Joseph Smith.

During the winter of 1838–39, Joseph, Hyrum, and some others spent four cold, miserable months in Liberty Jail "surrounded with demons," as Joseph put it, "where we are compelled to hear nothing but blasphemous oaths, and witness a scene of blasphemy, and drunkenness and hypocrisy, and debaucheries of every description."[7] He and his fellow prisoners were taunted with boasts about how the Saints were suffering. In the midst of this affliction, the Prophet finally reached a point where he wondered why his pleas for help were going unanswered. He pleaded, "O God, where art thou? . . . Yea, O Lord, how long shall they suffer these wrongs and unlawful oppressions, before thine heart shall be softened toward them, and thy bowels be moved with compassion toward them?" (D&C 121:1, 3).

"Whenever these moments of our extremity come," says Elder Jeffrey R. Holland,

> we must not succumb to the fear that God has abandoned us or that He does not hear our prayers. He does hear us. He does see us. He does love us. When we are in dire circumstances and want to cry 'Where art Thou?' it is imperative that we remember He is right there with us—where He has always been! We must continue to believe, continue to have faith, continue to pray and plead with heaven, even if we feel for a time our prayers are not heard and that God has somehow gone away.[8]

The Spirit whispered comfort to the Prophet: "My son, peace be unto thy soul; thine adversity and thine afflictions shall be but a small moment; and then, if thou endure it well, God shall exalt thee on high" (D&C 121:7–8). Sometimes life knocks us down, and when we get up, it knocks us down again. The Lord allows such adversity to try us so that we may grow spiritually and become like Him.

Elder Holland adds that while Joseph was "falsely accused, . . . torn away from his family and cast into a pit, into the hands of murderers, nevertheless, he was to remember that the same thing had happened to the Savior of the world, and because He was triumphant, so shall we be (see D&C 122:4–7)."[9] Elder Holland then testifies that "the path of salvation has always led one way or another through

Gethsemane. So if the Savior faced such injustices and discourage-ments, such persecutions, unrighteousness, and suffering, we cannot expect that we are not going to face some of that if we still intend to call ourselves His true disciples and faithful followers."[10]

A Refiner's Fire

Three years after the experience at Liberty Jail, the Prophet described the Lord as "a refiner's fire" who will purify us and purge us "as gold and silver" (D&C 128:24). In other words, the Lord is like a metalworker who holds our souls, like impure ore, close to the fire in order to burn away the dross.

Today, in our wiser moments, we choose to be "sanctified from all unrighteousness" so that we might be "prepared for the celestial glory" (D&C 88:18). In this purifying process, we can have faith that the Master is carefully watching. As a metalworker refines ore, he knows it is ready when he can see his image reflected in it. And so it is with us. We place our hope in Christ, believing that we shall be like Him when He comes again, "purified even as he is pure" (Moroni 7:48). Then, sanctified by the Spirit, we will reflect His image in our countenances.

> When through the deep waters I call thee to go,
> The rivers of sorrow shall not thee o'erflow,
> For I will be with thee, thy troubles to bless,
> And sanctify to thee thy deepest distress.
>
> When through fiery trials thy pathways shall lie,
> My grace, all sufficient, shall be thy supply;
> The flame shall not hurt thee; I only design
> Thy dross to consume, and thy gold to refine.[11]

If we endure our sufferings with patience, the Holy Ghost will refine us and sanctify us. May we cherish the companionship of the Holy Ghost, an old friend who warns of danger, speaks peace to our souls, and purifies and sanctifies us so that we might reflect the image of our Savior.

NOTES

1. Quoted by Dallin H. Oaks in "'Always Have His Spirit,'" *Ensign*, Nov. 1996, 60.
2. Packer, *Mine Errand from the Lord*, 122–23.
3. *Deseret Weekly*, September 5, 1891, 323; quoted in *Teachings of Presidents of the Church: Wilford Woodruff*, 46.
4. Barbara Jones Hadley, "Danger behind the Door," *New Era*, Oct. 1997, 49; used by permission.
5. Bonnie D. Parkin, "My Portrait of Jesus: A Work in Progress," in *To Save the Lost: An Easter Celebration* (Provo, UT: Religious Studies Center, Brigham Young University, 2009), 89.
6. Brigham Young, in *Juvenile Instructor*, July 19, 1873, 114.
7. Joseph Smith, *History of the Church of Jesus Christ of Latter-day Saints*, ed. B. H. Roberts, 2nd ed. rev. (Salt Lake City: Deseret Book, 1957), 3:290.
8. Jeffrey R. Holland, "Lessons from Liberty Jail," *BYU Magazine*, Winter 2009, 36.
9. Ibid., 37.
10. Ibid.
11. Robert Keen, "How Firm a Foundation," *Hymns*, no. 85.

6. The Gifts of the *Spirit*

"To every man is given a gift by the Spirit of God."
—DOCTRINE AND COVENANTS 46:11

Those who have been baptized and confirmed members of the Church are invited to "receive the Holy Ghost." In addition to the marvelous gift of the Holy Ghost, we are invited to seek other gifts of the Spirit. The Lord counsels, "Seek ye earnestly the best gifts, always remembering for what they are given" (D&C 46:8). They are given to us "to give us strength, lead us to do good, help us resist temptation, encourage and edify us, increase our wisdom, help us judge righteously, and help us qualify for eternal life."[1] In other words, they are gifts from a loving God who wants to help us on our journey home.

The diversity of gifts in a ward or branch makes each member valuable. We are all enriched when members contribute their gifts or talents, but we are diminished when someone holds back or refuses to contribute. As the poet John Ruskin wrote, "The weakest among us has a gift, however seemingly trivial, which is peculiar to him and which worthily used will be a gift also to his race."[2]

Variety of Spiritual Gifts

Elder Bruce R. McConkie claimed that "spiritual gifts are endless in number and infinite in variety," adding that "those listed in the revealed word are simply illustrations of the boundless outpouring of divine grace that a gracious God gives those who love and serve him."[3] Though spiritual gifts are endless in number, the following are a few important gifts that guide and strengthen us on our journey home:

• *The Light of Christ (see Moroni 7:18).* When we are born, we receive the Light of Christ, or conscience, to guide us throughout our lives (see Moroni 7:16). This divine influence helps us choose the right and "learn again the truths that we knew in our premortal existence but have forgotten in mortality."[4] Heavenly Father loves all of His children, and He wants them not only to live good lives but also come to the fullness of the gospel of Jesus Christ. Nevertheless, He blesses them according to the light they are willing to receive.

• *The gift of charity (see Moroni 7:46).* We receive the gift of charity by praying to the Father "with all the energy of heart" (Moroni 7:48). This gift is called the greatest of all because although people may have other gifts—the gift of speaking in tongues, the gift of prophecy, and an understanding of the mysteries of the kingdom—if they lack charity, the Lord says they are nothing (see 1 Corinthians 13:1–3). We have all known people who were extremely talented but were very impatient with others. I believe that some of the true marks of discipleship are the kindness and patience we show to each other.

• *The gift of hope (see Moroni 8:26).* President Dieter F. Uchtdorf wrote, "Hope is a gift of the Spirit." He then explained, "To all who suffer—to all who feel discouraged, worried, or lonely—I say with love and deep concern for you, never give in. Never surrender. Never allow despair to overcome your spirit. Embrace and rely upon the Hope of Israel, for the love of the Son of God pierces all darkness, softens all sorrow, and gladdens every heart."[5] I believe the gift of hope is centered in Christ and in the belief that we can be forgiven and resurrected through the power of His infinite Atonement.

• *The gift of teaching (see Moroni 10:9).* The First Presidency counsels that to become better teachers, we should use the resources given to us, including *Teaching, No Greater Call.* They ask us to devote our "best efforts to the teaching and rearing of . . . children in gospel principles which will keep them close to the Church."[6] The gift of teaching ignites the power of faith in the hearers, much as a lit match ignites another match.

• *The gift of great faith (see Moroni 10:11).* Faith is a key that unlocks many other spiritual gifts, such as the gift of healing (the topic of our next chapter). Without faith, no other gifts are given. In a stern message to the world, Moroni warns that spiritual gifts will be done away if we lack faith: "And now I speak unto all the ends of the earth—that if the day cometh that the power and gifts of God shall be done away among you, it shall be because of unbelief. And wo be unto the children of men if this be the case; for there shall be none that doeth good among you, no not one. For if there be one among you that doeth good, he shall work by the power and gifts of God" (Moroni 10:24–25).

• *The gift of testimony (see D&C 46:13).* This gift will wither unless we nurture it with faith, prayer, and repentance. As we nurture our testimony as a tender plant, it will take root and grow day by day until it matures into the tree bearing the fruit of eternal life (see Alma 32:26–43). Without frequent watering (prayer and scripture study), our testimony will fade.

• *The gift of wisdom (see D&C 46:17).* Although we may gain great knowledge of the gospel of Jesus Christ, it does us little good unless we are willing to apply those truths. Even devils know that Jesus is the Christ, but they do not act on that knowledge. The gift of wisdom also refers to good judgment, according to Elder Dallin H. Oaks.[7] Applied knowledge is vital to our salvation. We must not only talk the talk but also walk the walk.

• *The gift of knowledge (see D&C 46:18).* The Lord says that if we gain knowledge and intelligence in this life through our diligence and obedience, we will have the greater advantage in the world to come (see D&C 130:19). He invites us to learn about the heavens, the earth, and all things that are in them, including history and political events both at home and abroad (see D&C 88:78–79). Latter-day Saints are as committed to seeking higher education as any other group I have ever seen.

• *The gift of speaking in or interpreting tongues (see D&C 46:24–25).* This gift blesses the worldwide Church as members and missionaries learn new languages or, less commonly, are blessed to communicate instantly in another language. The Prophet Joseph Smith teaches, "Tongues were given for the purpose of preaching among those whose language is not understood; as on the day of Pentecost, etc., and it is not necessary for tongues to be taught to the Church particularly, for any man that has the Holy Ghost can speak of the things of God in his own tongue as well as to speak in another; for faith comes not by signs, but by hearing the word of God."[8] In other words, the gift of tongues is unlikely to be manifested unless it has a purpose: to communicate the word of God to those who need to hear it in another language.

• *The gift of prophecy (see D&C 46:22).* This gift refers more to teaching about the Savior and His gospel than to predicting future events, though sometimes the latter does occur. The Bible Dictionary notes that prophets may foretell, but in most cases they serve as "a forthteller rather than a foreteller."[9] Our latter-day prophets, seers, and revelators lead the way in both of these significant gifts.

• *The gift of discernment (see D&C 46:27).* This gift guides priesthood leaders to discern the proper use of spiritual gifts, especially by those who pretend to use them but who are "not of God" (D&C 46:27). This gift is important for our leaders because Satan desires to lead us astray with counterfeits of spiritual gifts (see D&C 50:2–3).

• *Other gifts and talents.* A loving Father in Heaven gives every person a gift, and it is a tragedy when people think they have no gifts or talents. "For us to conclude that we have no gifts when we judge ourselves by stature, intelligence, grade-point average, wealth, power, position, or external appearance is not only unfair, but unreasonable," Elder Marvin J. Ashton said. "It is up to each of us to search for and build upon the gifts which God has given." Among these gifts not listed in the scriptures are

> the gift of asking; the gift of listening; the gift of hearing and using a still, small voice; the gift of being able to weep; the gift of avoiding contention; the gift of being agreeable; the gift of avoiding vain repetition; the gift of seeking that which is righteous; the gift of not passing judgment; the gift of looking to God for guidance; the gift of being a disciple; the gift of caring for others; the gift of being able to ponder; the gift of offering prayer; the gift of bearing a mighty testimony; and the gift of receiving the Holy Ghost.[10]

I love this quote because it suggests the infinite variety of gifts that we can receive—if we will seek them.

Seeking Spiritual Gifts

I believe we often live beneath our privileges in the area of seeking spiritual gifts. The Lord is waiting to grant us these gifts if we will:

- Ask for such gifts "in the Spirit" (D&C 46:30).
- "Practice virtue and holiness before [Him] continually" (D&C 46:33).
- Use these gifts to serve others (see D&C 46:12, 26).
- Thank God "for whatsoever blessing [we] are blessed with" (D&C 46:32).
- Use these gifts "in the name of Christ" (D&C 46:31).

It is my prayer that we will identify those gifts that we have already received and seek earnestly the greater gifts God has in store.

NOTES

1. Mervyn B. Arnold, "Messages from the Doctrine and Covenants: Seek Ye Earnestly the Best Gifts," *Ensign*, Mar. 2005, 65.
2. Quoted in *The Book of Positive Quotations*, 334.
3. Bruce R. McConkie, *A New Witness for the Articles of Faith* (Salt Lake City: Deseret Book, 1985), 371.
4. Joseph B. Wirthlin, "The Unspeakable Gift," *Ensign*, May 2003, 26.
5. Dieter F. Uchtdorf, "The Infinite Power of Hope," *Ensign*, Nov. 2008, 24.
6. First Presidency letter, February 11, 1999.
7. Dallin H. Oaks, "Spiritual Gifts," *Ensign*, Sept. 1986, 69.
8. *Teachings of the Prophet Joseph Smith*, comp. Joseph Fielding Smith (Salt Lake City: Deseret Book, 1976), 148–49.
9. LDS Bible Dictionary, "Prophet," 754.
10. Marvin J. Ashton, "'There Are Many Gifts,'" *Ensign*, Nov. 1987, 20.

7. The Gift of *Healing*

"Thy faith hath made thee whole."
—MATTHEW 9:22

The Savior's power is real and available to us in mortality. He hears our anguished cries and will succor us in our afflictions. Whether we are feeling the grief of losing a loved one, the sadness that comes from sin, or even simple mortal mistakes, physical and spiritual healing are available to us through the touch of the Master's hand.

The poem "The Touch of the Master's Hand" tells of a master violinist who picks up a battered, old instrument considered worthless by a thoughtless crowd. Despite the flaws of the instrument, the violinist is able to bring forth a melody as sweet as the angels sing.

> And many a man with life out of tune,
> And battered and scarred with sin,
> Is auctioned cheap to the thoughtless crowd,
> Much like the old violin. . . .
> But the Master comes, and the foolish crowd
> Never can quite understand
> The worth of a soul and the change that's wrought
> By the touch of the Master's hand.[1]

Miracles in Ancient Times

The Lord devoted much of His mortal ministry to healing people. He not only exercised the power to heal but also gave this gift to His disciples, telling them to share this gift of healing freely (see Matthew 10:8).

It is significant that Jesus often touched people to heal them, even lepers, who were considered unclean and therefore untouchable. Although He could have worked miracles without touching the sick and afflicted, He often chose to employ a method involving personal connection and intimacy.

One father heard of the Master Healer and asked the disciples for help. His son frequently fell on the ground, foaming at the mouth and convulsing. After the disciples tried unsuccessfully to heal the son, the father pleaded for help from Jesus. Jesus replied, "If thou canst believe, all things are possible to him that believeth." Then the father pleaded tearfully, "Help thou mine unbelief" (Mark 9:23–24). When Jesus commanded the spirit to depart, the boy fell as one dead, but Jesus took him by the hand, and he was healed.

The disciples, amazed at this miracle and puzzled as to why they were unable to help the boy, asked, "Why could we not cast him out?"

Jesus answered, "This kind can come forth by nothing, but by prayer and fasting" (Mark 9:28–29). Clearly, fasting and prayer are vital elements to strengthening our faith to heal or be healed.

Some people were healed simply by touching the Master. Luke recorded the instance of a woman who had an issue of blood. Perhaps once well-to-do, she had "spent all her living upon physicians" (Luke 8:43). With her issue of blood, she would have been considered unclean by society. The woman represented "depletion in nearly every way—physically, socially, financially, and emotionally—but not spiritually," according to Camille Fronk Olson. "In the midst of all her distress, buried in the impossibility of her circumstance, she had one shining hope. With a boldness and determination that must have stretched her weakened body to its limits, the woman crafted a means to access her Savior without anyone's notice. Accustomed to being invisible to society and likely reduced to living near the ground, the woman reached out to touch the border of the Savior's robe as he passed by."[2] In the midst of the multitude, Jesus felt the power of her faith as she was healed. He called her "daughter," and offered words of hope: "Be of good comfort" (Luke 8:48). What physicians could not heal, Christ could heal.

Just as He did in the Old World, Christ performed similar miracles in the New World. He spent hours allowing the twenty-five hundred men, women, and children to touch His wounds in His hands, feet, and side. Ponder how they would have felt while you take the sacrament. Think about Christ's Atonement. "*Come . . . unto me*," He says, "that ye may *feel* the prints of the nails in my hands and in my feet, that ye may *know* that I am the God of Israel, and the God of the whole earth" (3 Nephi 11:14; emphasis added). Each Sunday as we partake of the sacrament, we *come* unto Him, *feel* the power of His Atonement, and *know* that He is our Savior.

As that first day of His visit to the Americas drew to a close, He invited the sick and afflicted to come unto Him and be healed (see 3 Nephi 17:9). These miracles testified that He was the God of the whole earth and had miraculous power to heal them.

Healing in Modern Times

Wouldn't it be wonderful to feel His hands on our heads as He healed us? In a sense, we do feel His healing touch as prayers are offered in our behalf or when righteous priesthood holders lay their hands on our heads and speak in His name and by His authority. President Gordon B. Hinckley testified, "As members of the Church of Jesus Christ, ours is a ministry of healing, with a duty to bind the wounds and ease the pain of those who suffer. Upon a world afflicted with greed and contention, upon families distressed by argument and selfishness, upon individuals burdened with sin and troubles and sorrows, I invoke the healing power of Christ, giving my witness of its efficacy and wonder."[3] The day of miracles has not passed. Miracles of both physical and spiritual healing still occur today.

In 2008 my daughter's high school cross-country team traveled to Los Angeles for a meet, and I went along as a chaperone. The December sunshine warmed us all, and we were in high spirits. We ran the course and went back to the pool for a swim. The students had a great time swimming and later decided to have a "chicken fight," with one student perched on the shoulders of another. While I was soaking in the hot tub, I suddenly saw one of the boys being dragged from the water. His face was pale, and his legs had no strength. He was barely conscious, and we helped him lie down on a deck chair.

"What happened?" several people asked.

Logan, one of the boys, answered that he had seen the boy floating in the pool and assumed he was just playing around. He then grabbed him and said, "Charles, stop goofing off!" When Logan lifted him by the waist, Charles gasped for air—he had been unable to breathe.

When the coaches asked him questions, he could not talk or

respond normally. Every response came sluggishly. He had hit his head and experienced either a concussion or neck injury. When I asked him to squeeze my hand, he grimaced and barely applied any pressure.

We called 911, and the paramedics soon arrived. Charles was still slow to respond, and the paramedics put on a neck brace and carefully placed him on a stretcher. Concerned, many of his teammates asked how he was doing. We explained the situation and asked them to pray for him.

A few anxious hours passed before we heard from the hospital that not only was Charles fully responsive but he was also cleared to run his 5K race in the morning! We were amazed at his speedy recovery and pleasantly surprised when he ran his personal best on an extremely challenging, hilly course.

In a testimony meeting the next day, Charles recognized the miracle of his healing, and we wept silently as he acknowledged the hand of the Lord.

Enduring in Faith

Sometimes, as with Charles, healing comes quickly. More often, it takes time, even with medical help. For example, recently my friend John noticed that he was weary all the time. Each day when he came home from his job as a hospital administrator, he was worn out and wanted only to sleep.

His wife noticed how tired he was and wondered what was wrong. Feeling fatigued, he tried to put on a brave face and continue to be a good husband and father. He served faithfully in his calling, but felt buried in a pit of discouragement. His family and coworkers asked what was wrong. His loving wife wanted to support him in his trials but did not know what to do to help him. Something felt deeply amiss.

He prayerfully sought the counsel of priesthood holders. As they fasted and prayed together for an answer, his stake president promised he would find a resolution to the problem and said, under the influence of the Spirit, that it was imperative that he identify the source of the problem.

Medical tests revealed no abnormalities, so John decided to press forward and keep serving and praying for help. Despite his discouragement, he carried on in his employment and chose to attend the temple weekly with his stake president, who remained close to the situation.

After a period of months, doctors speculated that a new medication might help. The family prayed that this might be the long-awaited solution they had been hoping for.

Following a month or more of treatment, he did not seem to be any better off than he was before. Disappointed, he told his wife he longed to return to his heavenly home.

"It's not time to go," she quietly insisted.

Finally, help came from "an angel," he said, "but not of the heavenly variety." A nurse at his workplace insisted that he get more tests. They showed that he had a quarter-sized hole in his heart. The faulty heart was circulating blood that did not have the impurities removed, so this was causing systemic weakness.

After surgery, his heart was repaired and he regained the energy and vitality that he had once enjoyed. In gratitude, he thanked his family for not giving up on him. He thanked the nurse for being inspired enough to insist that he get another test. And he thanked the physicians—and more particularly, the Master Physician—for healing his heart.

When Healing Does Not Come

President Packer testifies that Christ "is the Master Healer, the Master Counselor, the Master Comforter. There is no hurt He cannot soothe, no rejection He cannot assuage, no loneliness He cannot console, and no weakness He cannot strengthen. Whatever affliction the world casts at us, He has a remedy of superior healing power."[4] Still, there are times when it is not the Lord's will for someone to be healed.

Elder M. Russell Ballard shared the story of how his family watched helplessly as his four-month-old granddaughter struggled to live. They united in prayer and sought the will of the Lord in this matter. Elder Ballard personally knelt in prayer to seek direction. At the hospital, he said, "[When] I took my tiny little grandchild's hand and looked at her, I felt the Savior's touch. Into my mind came the words, as though spoken by her to me, 'Don't worry, Grandpa; I'll be all right.' Peace came into my heart. The Master's touch fell upon all of us."[5] The baby died soon afterward, but the family was prepared for that loss and comforted by the power of the Spirit.

Lest we become discouraged when healing does not come, the Lord has counseled us, "He that hath faith in me to be healed, and is not appointed unto death, shall be healed" (D&C 42:48). It is clear that sometimes loved ones are appointed unto death, and even death can be considered a release from pain and suffering—even, in a sense, a healing. "Who would want to live in their world, in this mortal condition, forever, with all the pain and the suffering and the anguish of soul that come?" asked President Joseph Fielding Smith. "None of us would wish it, and especially if we understood that this is only a temporary probation and that by passing on we should come to a glorious condition of eternal life. We would not want to stay here."[6]

The idea that a loved one is free from the pains of mortality does not lessen the grief we feel when we "weep for the loss of them that die" (D&C 42:45). Still, we take assurance from the Lord's promise that those who die in Him "shall not taste of death, for it shall be sweet unto them" (D&C 42:46). The ultimate healing, of course, does not occur until the Resurrection, when we will rise again with glorified, perfected bodies—healed by the touch of the Master's hand.

NOTES

1. Myra Brooks Welch, "The Touch of the Master's Hand," in *Best-Loved Poems of the LDS People,* 183.

2. Camille Fronk Olson, "They Ministered unto Him of Their Substance," in *To Save the Lost: An Easter Celebration,* 73.

3. Gordon B. Hinckley, "The Healing Power of Christ," *Ensign,* Nov. 1988, 59.

4. Tad R. Callister, "Teaching the Atonement," in *Teach One Another Words of Wisdom: Selections from the Religious Educator,* ed. Richard Neitzel Holzapfel and David M. Whitchurch (Provo, UT: Religious Studies Center, Brigham Young University, 2009), 39–40.

5. M. Russell Ballard, "The Divine Touch," *New Era,* Dec. 2004, 45.

6. Smith, *Selections from Doctrines of Salvation,* 53.

8. The Gift of *Forgiveness*

"He that repents and does the commandments of God shall be forgiven."
—DOCTRINE AND COVENANTS 1:32

What hope we feel in knowing that we can be forgiven! Without the hope of forgiveness granted by the Atonement of Jesus Christ, we would remain forever in our sins, shut out from God's presence, because no unclean thing can enter the kingdom of God.

"We all make mistakes," says President Packer. "Sometimes we harm ourselves and seriously injure others in ways that we alone cannot repair. We break things that we alone cannot fix. It is then in our nature to feel guilt and humiliation and suffering, which we alone cannot cure. That is when the healing power of the Atonement will help."[1]

Alma the Younger felt both the agony of sin and the sweet freedom of being released from the chains of death. As a rebellious young man, Alma went out with the sons of Mosiah to undermine the message of the gospel and to destroy the Church. These high-profile "anti-missionaries" were essentially apostates led by the prophet's own son and the children of the civic leader. Then an angel spoke to Alma with a voice that shook the earth, and Alma said, "I was racked with eternal torment, for my soul was harrowed up to the greatest degree and racked with all my sins" (Alma 36:12).

To be racked is to be afflicted or tormented, a powerful expression of the depths of his pain. He felt he had murdered many of God's children by leading them away from the truth. A harrow is a sharp plow that breaks up the soil to prepare it for seeds. This image is especially meaningful when you consider Alma's discourse on planting the seed in our hearts (see Alma 32:28). Alma's heart had to be broken in order to plant the seed of eternal life.

Fortunately, Alma remembered his father's teachings about the Atonement of Jesus Christ. "The doctrine of the Atonement is like a good seed planted in the ground," said Elder Tad R. Callister. "If, however, the seed is not nourished and taught in an atmosphere of spirituality, gratitude, and testimony, it will never bloom in the eye of the beholder."[2]

Placing his trust in the Son of God, Alma cried out, "O Jesus, thou Son of God, have *mercy* on me, who am in the gall of bitterness, and am encircled about by the everlasting chains of death" (Alma 36:18; emphasis added). His faith in Jesus Christ and the Atonement then delivered Alma from death. "And now, behold, when I thought this," he continued, "I could remember my pains no more; yea, I was harrowed up by the memory of my sins no more. And oh, what joy, and what marvelous light I did behold; yea, my soul was filled with joy as exceeding as was my pain!" (Alma 36:19–20). Although Alma had suffered intense grief and pain during the repentance process, he found great joy and release from suffering through the Atonement of Christ.

If Thy Right Hand Offend Thee

Serious sins require serious repentance. A story illustrates the high cost of freedom paid by one hiker who strayed off the beaten path. Twenty-seven-year-old Colorado mountain climber Aron Ralston went on a solo hike in Utah's Blue John Canyon without telling others where he was headed. While scrambling through the canyon, he accidentally dislodged an eight-hundred-pound boulder that crushed his right hand and forearm, trapping him with its immense weight. Unable to free himself, he gulped water from his bottle. In horror, he realized that he had drained one-third of his water supply and needed to ration the rest till help arrived. Waiting in agony, Aron lived for six days on his meager supply of two burritos, a chocolate muffin, five chocolate bars, and a little water.

After thinking long and hard about his options, he decided to do the unthinkable: amputate his own right arm using a dull, Leatherman-type knife blade. He survived the ordeal—but at a great cost.[3]

Sometimes we feel trapped by an eight-hundred-pound boulder. Caught between a rock and a hard place, we look for help, which seems nowhere to be found. Finally, we realize the price of freedom: "And if thy right hand offend thee, cut it off, and cast it from thee: for it is profitable for thee that one of thy members should perish, and not that thy whole body should be cast into hell" (Matthew 5:30).

Elder Dallin H. Oaks asked, "Why is it necessary for us to suffer on the way to repentance for serious transgressions?" He then answered in terms of an analogy:

A person who sins is like a tree that bends easily in the wind. On a windy and rainy day, the tree bends so deeply against the ground that the leaves become soiled with mud, like sin. If we focus only on cleaning the leaves, the weakness in the tree that allowed it to bend and soil its leaves may remain. Similarly, a person who is merely sorry to be soiled by sin will sin again in the next high wind. The susceptibility to repetition continues until the tree has been strengthened.[4]

Trapped by Sin

The following is a true story of a young man who struggled with an addiction. For many months, Sean's parents saw signs that something was wrong with their son, but what was it? He was normally respectful but lately had been acting moody and sarcastic. He procrastinated doing his homework and resisted doing chores. Usually a straight-A student, he failed a class and didn't seem to care. Then, after attending a session of general conference, he told his father he had been viewing pornography for over several months. He had become numb to the situation and almost past feeling (see Ephesians 4:19). He had become distant to the point that little else mattered but his next encounter.

Fortunately, he realized his life had fallen out of tune, and he had the courage to confess. Interviews with a loving bishop and a professional counselor helped Sean put his life back in harmony again.

At first Sean said he wanted to change, but his heart did not seem to be in it. He had been experimenting for fun, but he soon realized how hard it was to change. He kept returning to old habits and became defensive when asked about his progress. "Hey, I have the right to make my own choices, don't I? And I'm glad!" he once said angrily. It is common for people with serious addictions to confuse their priorities and feel that nothing else matters.[5] Like ink in water, sin had clouded his perspective on life.

As time passed, he increasingly wanted to put sin behind him, but he felt trapped. Ironically, while he was immersed in sin, he felt numb in other areas of his life. Now that he was beginning to repent, he began to feel again—and to feel deeply. Harrowed up by his sins, he felt the deep sorrow of a broken heart. In hindsight, he saw that "wickedness never was happiness" (Alma 41:10). Memories of his past haunted him. He realized how depressed he had been during that time. Short-term pleasure took away the numbness, confusion, and pain he felt in his life, but it was a fleeting release.

Steps in the Right Direction

Sean talked privately with his father, his bishop, and a professional counselor in order to gain a new perspective on his sin and loneliness and to begin healing the wounds of sin. He formed positive, achievable goals, such as preparing himself to attend the temple someday. He began forming an escape plan when his mind began to center on unhealthy thoughts (see 1 Corinthians 10:13).

Journal writing proved to be a valuable part of the repentance process. He asked himself what needs he had felt that had led him to seek solace in addiction. He identified the fact that he felt socially awkward, and this loneliness led him to seek happiness in unhealthy fantasies. He realized that he felt a deep, underlying sadness relieved by acting out on those impulses. Part of his desire for short-term pleasure stemmed from his loneliness. To remedy this, he began building stronger friendships and planning fun, wholesome activities with his friends.

The decisive moment was when Sean chose to follow his bishop's counsel to fast and pray for spiritual strength to overcome temptation. Like Alma, he sought the power of Christ to help him break the chains of death (see Alma 36:18). "What must I do to break the chains that bind me and lead me away from the path our Savior would have us follow?" asked Elder Marvin J. Ashton. "These chains cannot be broken by those who live in lust and self-deceit. They can only be broken by people who are willing to change. We must face up to the hard reality of life that damaging chains are broken only by people of courage and commitment who are willing to struggle and weather the pain."[6]

The Healing Process

The seeds of change had been planted in his heart, but they needed time and nurturing to grow. This process would take many months of soul-searching, fasting, and prayer. Despite his steps in the right direction, Sean often felt discouraged by his slow progress. In a recent devotional, Elder Bruce C. Hafen described the challenges of overcoming the "natural man" by sketching a rocket trying to escape the pull of earth's gravity. The "gravitational pull of darkness" keeps us down as we are trying to escape the influence of the world. Fortunately, as we begin to escape that pull, other forces begin to help us along. In this example, as the rocket escapes earth's gravity, it is then acted on by forces representing the Father's own gravitational pull.[7]

Sean found protective power in reading just before going to bed and just after rising in the morning. He began to take hope as he read about the saving effects of the Atonement in the scriptures, *The Infinite Atonement*, and *The Miracle of Forgiveness*. He prayed with greater intensity to experience a mighty change of heart. "This mighty change," says Elder David A. Bednar, "is not simply the result of working harder or developing greater individual discipline. Rather, it is the consequence of a fundamental change in our desires, our motives, and our natures made possible through the Atonement of Christ the Lord." He was learning to overcome "both sin and the desire to sin, both the taint and the tyranny of sin."[8] Over a long period, Sean realized that sin was no longer as attractive as it had once seemed. His heart was being sanctified by the Spirit.

After many months, Sean was encouraged by his progress and began to radiate the Savior's love. He became again as a little child, willing to submit to anything the Lord asked. He found that "there is no habit, no addiction, no rebellion, no transgression, no apostasy, no crime exempted from the promise of complete forgiveness. That is the promise of the atonement of Christ."[9]

Extending the Gift to Others

Of course, forgiveness is a gift that we want for ourselves, but the Lord requires us to extend this same gift to others. The Lord's Prayer emphasizes this: "If ye forgive men their trespasses, your heavenly Father will also forgive you" (Matthew 6:14).

Why does Heavenly Father grant us forgiveness "measure for measure"? To put this into earthly terms, imagine ourselves, children of God, as squabbling siblings who sulk and are irrational in our hatred. A loving father sees that we are blinded by our anger and then calms us down so we can apologize. Then we have to let it go.

In fact, forgiving another may be the greatest gift we can give ourselves.

- *Visualize untying yourself.* The Aramaic word for "forgive" means to untie. The fastest way to free yourself from the chains of bondage is to forgive your enemy.

- *Stop telling the story.* How many times a day do you think about how badly you were hurt? How many times a week do you retell the story? Forgiving someone is the kindest thing you can do for your friends and family.

- *Tell the story from the other person's perspective.* Imagine that you are the person who offended you and use the word "I" when saying what that person would say. Changing your perspective this way is not easy, but it holds great power.

- *Replace negative thoughts with well wishes.* The Savior taught, "Love your enemies, bless them that curse you, do good to them that hate you, and pray for them which despitefully use you, and persecute you" (Matthew 5:44). Sincerely praying for the person who hurt you will have the effect of neutralizing the acid that would harm you.

- *Be patient.* If you have thought about a problem for a long time, it will take some time to change directions. Be patient and kind to yourself. Don't bottle up the pain. Give yourself time to heal—physically and emotionally.[10]

I personally testify that forgiveness brings peace and release from the pain of anger and heartache.

Forgiving a Friend

It is difficult to forgive an enemy, but it is even more difficult to forgive a friend who has hurt us. An example of this is William W.

Phelps, a convert to the Church who served in the stake presidency in Missouri. When he was accused of financial indiscretions in Missouri, he was excommunicated and he became embittered, signing a petition to have the Saints removed from the state.

Many suffered severely because of Brother Phelps's actions, but in 1840, he wrote a letter asking forgiveness of Brother Joseph and the Saints. Brother Joseph wrote:

> You may in some measure realize what my feelings, as well as Elder Rigdon's and Brother Hyrum's were, when we read your letter—truly our hearts were melted into tenderness and compassion when we ascertained your resolves, etc. I can assure you I feel a disposition to act on your case in a manner that will meet the approbation of Jehovah, (whose servant I am), and agreeable to the principles of truth and righteousness which have been revealed; and inasmuch as long-suffering, patience, and mercy have ever characterized the dealings of our heavenly Father towards the humble and penitent, I feel disposed to copy the example, cherish the same principles, and by so doing be a savior of my fellow men.
>
> It is true, that we have suffered much in consequence of your behavior—the cup of gall, already full enough for mortals to drink, was indeed filled to overflowing when you turned against us, one with whom we had oft taken sweet counsel together, and enjoyed many refreshing seasons from the Lord—'had it been an enemy, we could have borne it.' . . .
>
> However, the cup has been drunk, the will of our Father has been done, and we are yet alive, for which we thank the Lord. And having been delivered from the hands of wicked men by the mercy of our God, we say it is your privilege to

be delivered from the powers of the adversary, be brought into the liberty of God's dear children, and again take your stand among the Saints of the Most High, and by diligence, humility, and love unfeigned, commend yourself to our God, and your God, and to the Church of Jesus Christ.

Believing your confession to be real, and your repentance genuine, I shall be happy once again to give you the right hand of fellowship, and rejoice over the returning prodigal.

Your letter was read to the Saints last Sunday, and an expression of their feeling was taken, when it was unanimously resolved, that W. W. Phelps should be received into fellowship.

"Come on, dear brother, since the war is past,

For friends at first, are friends again at last."[11]

No wonder Brother Phelps loved and respected the Prophet for his greatness of spirit!

After the Martyrdom, a grieving Brother Phelps penned the tribute, "Praise to the man who communed with Jehovah! Jesus anointed that Prophet and Seer."[12]

This spirit of reconciliation—to be embraced in the Savior's arms despite all we have done—is at the very heart of the gospel. Forgiveness through mercy, beyond the grasp of justice, is what we seek from our Heavenly Father. I testify of the power of forgiveness, a divine gift we both receive and extend to others.

NOTES

1. Packer, *Mine Errand from the Lord*, 42.
2. Callister, "Teaching the Atonement," 40.

3. For Aron Ralston's full story, see *Between a Rock and a Hard Place* (New York: Atria Books, 2004). I thank Brent R. Nordgren for the application of this story to the account in Matthew 5.

4. Dallin H. Oaks, "The Atonement and Faith," *Liahona*, Apr. 2008, 10.

5. LDS Family Services, *Addiction Recovery Program: A Guide to Addiction Recovery and Healing* (Salt Lake City: The Church of Jesus Christ of Latter-day Saints, 2005), v.

6. Marvin J. Ashton, " 'Shake Off the Chains with Which Ye Are Bound,' " *Ensign*, Nov. 1986, 15.

7. Bruce C. Hafen, "A Disciple's Journey, *BYU Magazine*, Summer 2008, 28.

8. David A. Bednar, "Clean Hands and a Pure Heart," *Ensign*, Nov. 2007, 82.

9. Boyd K. Packer, "The Brilliant Morning of Forgiveness," *Ensign*, Nov. 1995, 20.

10. These ideas are adapted from http://www.wikihow.com/Forgive.

11. *Teachings of Presidents of the Church: Joseph Smith* (Salt Lake City: The Church of Jesus Christ of Latter-day Saints, 2007), 400.

12. William W. Phelps, "Praise to the Man," *Hymns*, no. 27.

9. The Gift of Grace

"Cheer up your hearts . . . and remember, after ye are reconciled unto God, that it is only in and through the grace of God that ye are saved."

—2 NEPHI 10:23–24

When a family went boating in Lake Powell, they decided to beat the heat by going for a swim. Among the swimmers was the family's eighty-five-year-old grandfather, who donned an orange life vest and lowered himself into the water.

All went well until the end of the swim when the tired family members made their way to the boat, climbing the ladder one by one. The younger members were able to climb up just fine, but their elderly grandfather was so worn out that he could only hang on helplessly as the boat bobbed in the waves. Panicking, he gripped the ladder so tightly that no one could budge him.

Seeing the dilemma, his daughter called out, "Let go and reach up!" Sensing that he could do nothing to help himself, Grandpa decided to trust his daughter, let go, and reach upward. As he did so, strong hands hauled him to safety.

He sprawled breathlessly on the deck. "Thanks," he gasped after a few moments. "I don't know how much longer I could have lasted." Then, after catching his breath, he said, "You know, I wonder how many times in my life I have struggled and relied on my own powers when what I needed to do was let go and reach up for help from above."[1]

Let go and reach up for help from above. The concept is simple, but often we struggle in life when the best thing to do would be to look upward for help. Panicking as the winds and the waves of the world toss us to and fro, we lose hope. Despite all those seminary lessons or Church talks on the Savior's mercy, we sometimes worry that we have to make it back to heaven on our own. Like Peter on the Sea of Galilee, we take a few faltering steps and then start to sink, forgetting that Christ is waiting with outstretched arms to assist us.

Confused at the Grace

The Bible Dictionary teaches that grace is a "divine means of help or strength" and an "enabling power" that helps us to become exalted.[2] For centuries, Christian denominations have argued about the role of grace and works in salvation, but the truth is that both are necessary. Of course, we do not believe in "cheap grace" (confessing Jesus as Lord but not being reconciled to Him by keeping His commandments). Nor do we believe in salvation by good works (trying to earn our way into heaven). Grace and works are like scissor blades—both work together.

The devil tries to deceive many into focusing on either grace or works to the exclusion of the other. For example, C. S. Lewis said that the devil "sends errors into the world in pairs—pairs of opposites. . . . He relies on your extra dislike of the one error to draw you gradually into the opposite one. But do not let us be fooled. We have to keep our eyes on the goal and go straight through between both errors."[3]

Both grace and works are essential, for Nephi taught, "It is by *grace* that we are saved, after all we can *do*" (2 Nephi 25:23; emphasis added). These divine doctrines go hand in hand to save us, because "when the lifeguard stretches out a pole to the drowning swimmer, the swimmer must reach out and hold on if he desires to be rescued. Both the lifeguard and the swimmer must fully participate if the swimmer's life is to be saved. Likewise, works and grace are not opposing doctrines, as is so often portrayed. To the contrary, they are indispensable partners."[4] However, in order to receive the gift of grace, we must reach upward and pray for divine assistance.

One winter my stake president decided to go surfing on the north shore of Oahu. The waves were huge. He decided that even he, a *haole*, could get up on waves that big. And he did get up, but he crashed into the beach like a wet sock. The impact knocked the wind out of him and just about knocked him unconscious. Then, just as he gathered his breath, a wave knocked him down again. He was powerless to stand and realized with horror that he might die there.

Fortunately, two strong natives ran to him and hauled him to safety. He pointed out that life is like that. It will knock us down and then, when we try to stand up, knock us down again. That is the very time when we need the Savior the most—and the time that he will succor us in our afflictions. The word *succor* means "to run to," and I believe the Savior will run to us in our hour of need.

Amazing Grace

When I think of grace, the experience of John Newton comes to mind. Newton was the blind sea captain memorialized in the movie *Amazing Grace*. While sailing homeward on May 10, 1748, a dreadful storm arose, tossing the ship to and fro like a tiny boat. In despair, he prayed, "Lord, have mercy upon us." After the storm abated, he reflected on the higher power that had saved him. Thereafter Newton observed May 10 as the date of his conversion. He penned the words of the beloved Protestant hymn that tells the story of his conversion story:

> Thro' many dangers, toils and snares,
> I have already come;
> 'Tis grace has brought me safe thus far,
> And grace will lead me home.
>
> Amazing grace, how sweet the sound,
> That saved a wretch like me.
> I once was lost but now am found,
> Was blind, but now, I see.[5]

Like Newton, we all face the storms of life on our homeward voyage, and we all need the grace of God to rescue us.

My Grace Is Sufficient

Grace does not mean a free pass from our troubles. The Apostle Paul complained about having "a thorn in the flesh" and being buffeted by Satan. Three times the Apostle prayed that this temptation might be removed from him, but the voice of the Lord offered this counsel: "My grace is sufficient for thee: for my strength is made perfect in weakness" (2 Corinthians 12:7, 9). Through his weakness, the Apostle Paul was made strong. Perhaps the natural temptations of the flesh served to remind him that he was utterly dependent on the Savior for mercy.

The prophet Moroni worried that the Gentiles would mock

him because of his weakness in writing, but the Lord told him, "Fools mock, but they shall mourn; and my grace is sufficient for the meek" (Ether 12:26). The worldly-wise may scoff at the notion of God's grace, but the meek seek it with all their hearts.

The Lord then said to Moroni, "If men come unto me I will show unto them their weakness" (v. 27). Who wants to be shown their weakness? I certainly don't. Yet the Lord seems to think it is necessary. He continued to testify, "My grace is sufficient for all men that humble themselves before me; for if they humble themselves before me, and have faith in me, then will I make weak things become strong unto them" (v. 27). This is why it is important to see our weaknesses—the gift of feedback is the path to improvement.

Perfection in Christ

When Moroni wrote his final message in the Book of Mormon, he invited us to "come unto Christ, and be perfected in him." He then promised, "If ye shall deny yourselves of all ungodliness, and love God with all your might, mind and strength, then is his grace sufficient for you, that by his grace ye may be *perfect in Christ*" (Moroni 10:32; emphasis added).

It is important to clarify that our goal is perfection in Christ—not perfecting ourselves, not earning our way into heaven by 100 percent Church attendance, home or visiting teaching, or anything of the like. It means coming unto Christ, repenting of our sins, and loving God with all our hearts. In short, it means becoming as a child.

Elder Bruce R. McConkie taught: "We have to become perfect to be saved in the celestial kingdom. But nobody becomes perfect in this life. Only the Lord Jesus attained that state, and he had an advantage that none of us has. He was the Son of God, and he came into this life with a spiritual capacity and a talent and an inheritance that exceeded beyond all comprehension what any of the rest of us was born with."

He continues:

> Degree by degree and step by step we start out in the course to perfection with the objective of becoming perfect as God our Heavenly Father is perfect, in which eventuality we become inheritors of eternal life in his kingdom.
>
> As members of the Church, if we chart a course leading to eternal life; if we begin the process of spiritual rebirth, and are going in the right direction; if we chart a course of sanctifying our souls, and degree by degree are going in that direction; and if we chart a course of becoming perfect, and, step by step and phase by phase, are perfecting our souls by overcoming the world, then it is absolutely guaranteed—there is no question whatever about it—we shall gain eternal life. Even though we have spiritual rebirth ahead of us, perfection ahead of us, the full degree of sanctification ahead of us, if we chart a course and follow it to the best of our ability in this life, then when we go out of this life we'll continue in exactly that same course. We will no longer be subject to the passions and the appetites of the flesh. We will have passed successfully the tests of this mortal probation and in due course we'll get the fulness of our Father's kingdom—and that means eternal life in his everlasting presence.[6]

Victory in Christ

I love Stephen E. Robinson's parable of the bicycle. Brother Robinson shared how his daughter Sarah wanted to buy a bicycle and how he said if she saved up her pennies, one day she would have enough to buy one. Weeks later, Sarah brought her jar of pennies and, with great excitement, asked if they could go buy the bicycle. Dismayed, he realized that she had taken him at his word and saved her pennies—sixty-one of them.

As agreed, they went to the store, where she found the perfect bike. But she began to cry when she saw the price tag: it cost over a hundred dollars. Her goal was hopelessly out of reach. Comforting her, he said, "You give me everything you've got, the whole sixty-one cents, and a hug and a kiss, and this bike is yours."[7]

Another analogy explains our ultimate dependence on the Savior for victory. One night during his rookie season, Chicago Bulls player Stacey King scored just one point—a free throw—the night his teammate Michael Jordan scored sixty-nine points. After the Bulls won the victory, reporters asked King what he thought about scoring only one point. He answered, "I'll always remember the night Michael Jordan and I combined to score seventy points."[8]

That is how it is with the Christ: we offer our single free throw, and He takes us to victory. No wonder we "stand all amazed at the love Jesus offers" us. No wonder we are "confused at the grace that so fully he proffers" us. No wonder we will kneel and "adore at the mercy seat."[9]

NOTES

1. William B. Smart, *Messages for a Happier Life: Inspiring Essays from the Church News* (Salt Lake City: Deseret Book, 1989), 27–28.

2. Bible Dictionary, "Grace," 697.

3. C. S. Lewis, *Mere Christianity* (New York: Macmillan, 1960), 160.

4. Tad R. Callister, *The Infinite Atonement* (Salt Lake City: Deseret Book, 2000), 310.

5. Information from http://www.anointedlinks.com/amazing_grace.html.

6. Bruce R. McConkie, *Doctrines of the Restoration: Sermons and Writings of Bruce R. McConkie* (Salt Lake City: Bookcraft, 1998), 52.

7. Stephen E. Robinson, *Believing Christ: The Parable of the Bicycle and Other Good News* (Salt Lake City: Deseret Book, 1992), 42.

8. Adapted from http://www.streetsvilleunited.ca/pdfs/BattlingGiants.pdf.

9. Gabriel, "I Stand All Amazed," *Hymns*, no. 193.

10. The Gift of *Eternal Life*

"Eternal life . . . is the greatest of all the gifts of God."
—DOCTRINE AND COVENANTS 14:7

All of the gifts of God are supernal, surpassing any gifts we might exchange on earth. Still, one gift surpasses all the rest. This ultimate gift is called by the Lord Himself "the greatest of all the gifts of God" (D&C 14:7; see also 1 Nephi 15:36). In fact, this gift encompasses the rest of God's gifts because it is the central purpose of the plan of happiness. This gift is the gift of eternal life.

Eternal life means knowing the Father and the Son and becoming one with them (see John 17:3, 21). It means dwelling in God's presence as an eternal family in eternal glory (see D&C 130:2). It means becoming even as God is and receiving all that He has— "glory, and salvation, and honor, and immortality, and eternal life; kingdoms, principalities, and powers!" (D&C 128:23). It means becoming kings and queens, priests and priestesses—serving under the direction of our Father in Heaven to accomplish His work and glory, namely, "to bring to pass the immortality and eternal life of man" (Moses 1:39).

Eternal life means much more than living forever, for the Lord calls that state "immortality," a gift freely given to all people through the magnificent power of the Resurrection. Eternal life, however, is "the greatest of all the gifts of God," writes Elder McConkie, "for it is the kind, status, type, and quality of life that God himself enjoys. Thus those who gain eternal life receive exaltation; they are sons of God, joint-heirs with Christ, members of the Church of the Firstborn; they overcome all things, have all power, and receive the fulness of the Father."[1]

A Vision of Our Eternal Potential

On February 16, 1832, the Father opened the heavens to the Prophet Joseph Smith and Sidney Rigdon, who saw a vision while other eyewitnesses were present, including my ancestor Philo Dibble. The account, now canonized as Doctrine and Covenants 76, states that those who receive eternal life will be called

> the church of the Firstborn. They are they into whose hands the Father has given all things—they are they who are priests and kings, who have received of his fulness, and of his glory; and are priests of the Most High, after the order of Melchizedek, which was after the order of Enoch, which was after the order of the Only Begotten Son. Wherefore, as it is written, they are gods, even the sons of God—wherefore, all things are theirs, whether life or death, or things present, or things to come, all are theirs and they are Christ's, and Christ is God's. (D&C 76:54–59)

This is deep doctrine that the Prophet Joseph Smith shared with a congregation gathered at King Follett's funeral in Nauvoo:

> Here, then, is eternal life—to know the only wise and true God; and you have got to learn how to be gods yourselves,

and to be kings and priests to God, the same as all gods have done before you, namely, by going from one small degree to another, and from a small capacity to a great one; from grace to grace, from exaltation to exaltation, until you attain to the resurrection of the dead, and are able to dwell in everlasting burnings, and to sit in glory, as do those who sit enthroned in everlasting power."[2]

As with any child, we have the potential to become like our parents.

I love these inspired words of C. S. Lewis, who wrote of our eternal potential:

> It is a serious thing to live in a society of possible gods and goddesses, to remember that the dullest and most uninteresting person you talk to may one day be a creature which, if you saw it now, you would strongly be tempted to worship. . . . It is in the light of these overwhelming possibilities, it is with the awe and the circumspection proper to them, that we should conduct all our dealings with one another, all friendships, all loves, all play, all politics. There are no ordinary people. You have never talked to a mere mortal.[3]

The Fulness of the Father

Eternal life means becoming a joint-heir with Christ. The Savior says in John 14:2, "In my Father's kingdom are many mansions. . . . I go to prepare a place for you." Commenting on this verse, the Prophet Joseph Smith said it ought to read like this: " 'In my Father's kingdom are many kingdoms,' in order that ye may be heirs of God and joint-heirs with me."[4]

It is significant that even Jesus Christ, the Son of God, needed the gift of grace to receive of the fulness of the Father's glory, for "he received not of the fulness at the first, but received grace for grace" (D&C 93:12). In essence, we offer to the Father our gift (our free will, or agency) for His divine gift (the enabling, exalting power of grace). We read that Jesus continued "from grace to grace, until He received a fulness" (D&C 93:13). As Latter-day Saints, we understand the concept of receiving the fulness to mean becoming like the Father and receiving His glory. We rejoice that this marvelous promise extends to us as well. In our own humble way, if we will keep the Father's commandments, we grow each day, receiving "grace for grace" and eventually "of his fulness," becoming glorified in the Son as the Son is in the Father (see D&C 93:20). By growing in faith, repenting of our sins, and freely offering our gift of agency to obey God, we become a little more like our Savior each day. "As many as believe in his name," says John, "shall receive of his fulness. And of his fulness have all we received, even immortality and eternal life, through his grace" (JST, John 1:16, Bible appendix).

We receive of the Father's fulness as we grow from grace to grace—exercising faith in Christ, accepting baptism by immersion for the remission of our sins, receiving the gift of the Holy Ghost and obeying His promptings, and then living up to our temple covenants.

Patience in the Journey

Sometimes we are discouraged by our slow progress on our journey home. The Prophet Joseph Smith offered the early Saints a sense of how long this journey will take. "When you climb up a ladder," he says, "you must begin at the bottom, and ascend step by step, until you arrive at the top, and so it is with the principles of the gospel—you must begin with the first, and go on until you learn all the principles of exaltation. But it will be a great while after you have passed through the veil before you will have learned them. It is not all to be comprehended in this world; it will be a great work to learn our salvation and exaltation even beyond the grave."[5]

Elder David A. Bednar added, "We will not attain a state of perfection in this life, but we can and should press forward with faith in Christ along the strait and narrow path and make steady progress toward our eternal destiny."[6] In other words, the direction we are traveling, not the speed, is what matters most.

We take hope, of course, in the small and steady incremental progress we make during our earthly sojourn. For example, think of a newborn infant. She can do very little but eat, cry, and mess her diaper. But then she grows up and increases in wisdom and knowledge, becoming at first a young woman and then perhaps a wife and mother. In the span of a few mortal years—the blink of an eye to our Father—this infant has become a mature and contributing woman.

With this eternal view, we hope that we can be transformed through the power of Christ into what our Maker intends for us. Regarding this process, President John Taylor wrote,

> It is for the exaltation of man to this state of superior intelligence and Godhead that the mediation and atonement of Jesus Christ is instituted; and that noble being, man, made in the image of God, is rendered capable not only of being a son of man, but also a son of God, . . . and is rendered capable of becoming a God, possessing the power, the majesty, the

exaltation and the position of a God. As it is written, "Beloved, now are we the sons of God, and it doth not yet appear what we shall be: but we know that, when he shall appear, we shall be like him; for we shall see him as he is" [1 John 3:2].[7]

Hope Offered in Holy Temples

This eternal perspective of our divine potential as children of God comes to us not only in the scriptures and the writings of modern prophets but also in holy temples. There we covenant to forsake sin and remain unspotted from the world. There we receive promises of our divine potential, that we may rule and reign under our Father's direction if we are faithful to our covenants. There we seek the peace of the Spirit and find quiet dignity to face the challenges of life.

I love this beautiful promise of the peace that comes with regular temple worship: "A temple is a retreat from the vicissitudes of life, a place of prayer and meditation providing an opportunity to receive inner peace, inspiration, guidance, and, frequently, solutions to the problems that vex our daily lives."[8] I testify that this is true.

For these reasons and many more, President Howard W. Hunter inspired us to "be a temple-attending and a temple-loving people," adding, "We should hasten to the temple as frequently, yet prudently, as our personal circumstances allow. . . . As we attend the temple, we learn more richly and deeply the purpose of life and the significance of the atoning sacrifice of the Lord Jesus Christ. Let us make the temple, with temple worship and temple covenants and temple marriage, our ultimate earthly goal and the supreme mortal experience."[9] The temple truly is the pinnacle of our earthly experience, and there we receive our greatest assurance of our eternal potential as children of God.

Conclusion

How grateful we are for the promise of eternal life. The assurance of this promise is the Holy Ghost, who comforts us as we press forward with a steadfastness in Christ, having a perfect brightness of hope and a love of God and of all mankind (see 2 Nephi 32:20).

This book ends, as it began, with a message of hope. Let us center our faith and trust in the Hope of Israel, our Savior Jesus Christ. His love "pierces all darkness, softens all sorrow, and gladdens every heart."[10] My hope and prayer is that all of us will press forward with a perfect brightness of hope until we lay hold of eternal life, this greatest of all gifts made possible through our Savior's love.

NOTES

1. McConkie, *Mormon Doctrine*, 237.
2. Smith, *History of the Church*, 6:306.
3. C. S. Lewis, *The Weight of Glory* (New York: HarperCollins, 2001), 14–15.
4. Smith, *History of the Church*, 6:365.
5. Ibid., 6:306–7.
6. Bednar, "Clean Hands and a Pure Heart," 82.
7. John Taylor, *The Mediation and Atonement* (Salt Lake City: Deseret News, 1892), 140–41.
8. Franklin D. Richards, "Happiness and Joy in Temple Work," *Ensign*, Nov. 1986, 70.
9. Howard W. Hunter, "A Temple-Motivated People," *Ensign*, Feb. 1995, 2.
10. Uchtdorf, "Infinite Power of Hope," 24.

About the Author

Devan Jensen has worked as executive editor at Brigham Young University's Religious Studies Center since 2001. He received his bachelor's and master's degree in English from Brigham Young University and has edited for Deseret Book, the Church Curriculum Department, and the *Ensign*. He and his wife, Patty, and four children live in Orem, Utah. His hobbies include biking, camping, hiking, magic tricks, movies, music, reading, Scouting, and sports.